THE GHOSTLY ASYL ᴀX

A paranc

by A.ᴀ

Copyrig.

Warning: This is an adults-only read due to ex.   .ve strong violence, supernatural description, cursing, sexual scenarios, demons, decapitation and torture, murder and much more - not for the easily shocked, squeamish or faint of heart.

When the past catches up with the present, angry spirits seek revenge. Can forces more powerful than they stop impending havoc? Time-travel through mirrors and portals in a haunted asylum, – built on a former church, centuries ago - evil demons, ghosts from the past, witches, murder, graphic decapitations and the harnessing of power by friends who try to solve a puzzle in order to banish it forever - this novel has it all, and lots more.

Staff at the asylum have company of a spectral kind who want something and are about to speak up after a long silence...

This is a work of fiction. Characters, places and incidents are from the author's vivid imagination. Any resemblance to real people, living or dead, or to places or incidents is purely coincidental.

~CHAPTER ONE~
A typical day in the asylum

Matron Williams - Claudia to her friends - wandered down the endless, eerie stone corridors of the asylum and browsed through the paperwork that contained her duties and responsibilities for that week. A voluptuous woman in her late forties, she wore a dark blue dress and a crisp, pristine white blouse underneath. Her knee-length tight black skirt skimmed her ample hips and thighs giving them the impression of being smaller than they actually were. Knowing that she wore black seamed stockings was her only pleasurable escapism from her monotonous daily duties. Black flat shoes finished off the stern-looking outfit and frequent frowns of stress finished off her equally stern-looking face which was framed by shoulder-length black wavy hair - with flecks of grey here and there.

A circular-shaped watch was pinned upside-down on her breast pocket for ease of access to the time. Her seamed black nylon stockings kept her legs toasty warm whenever she went downstairs to the basement area to chat with Bob, the security guard who was frequently found on night-shift - something that he detested due to the unusual activity that seemed to follow him around - which was ignored by his work colleagues who put it down to his wild imagination.

They possessed a certain jealousy and envy of him as he performed his work much more efficiently than *they* ever could. They often gossiped about him behind his back - assuming that he was quite deluded or just overtired as the incessant ramblings that he spouted; regarding ghostly activity and things grabbing him in the wee small hours - entertained them regularly. He however, knew only too well that what happened to him on a nightly basis, was far from an overactive imagination, fatigue or due to delusion. To him, it was very real - and did indeed occur. If only someone would listen to him, he often thought. But whenever he voiced his opinions, they fell on deaf ears, so, he learned to stop mentioning it and just got on with his job to the best of his ability.

He was a tall man; six-feet and four inches to be precise. He had to duck out of the way in time whenever walking under doorframes, otherwise he would receive bruising to the forehead frequently so he learned over the years to minimise that risk by hunching his shoulders automatically whenever the mere sight of a doorframe loomed toward him - which was often; due to the myriad of rooms within the huge asylum.

His colleagues had nicknamed him *Quasimodo* and they were often heard giggling whenever they saw him approaching. The look of bewilderment upon his face only added to their amusement. He had no idea why they mocked him and he had gone past caring what they thought of him. His responsibility was to ensure that the safety of everyone in the asylum was assured and, he remained vigilant in doing just that - daily.

The others had long ceased to venture down to the basement area after a terrifying incident that happened the day before. Not one of them had dared to discuss it...for fear of not being believed, or, for fear of being detained in the building as one of the patients! Bob knew that they believed that there was paranormal activity, but they were too gutless to admit it. Still, he got on with his work and that was all that mattered to him. A conscientious hard worker, he did an exemplary job and he knew it. Despite receiving regular praise from his superiors, he respected himself first and foremost and he took pride in his work. That was sufficient - for him.

Claudia liked Bob, and he liked her in return. They respected each other immensely. She patronised and scolded the other security guards for their shoddy attitude to their duties.

She often wondered what it would be like to be his wife, but she never let on that she had been harbouring feelings for him for quite some time now. He was fond of her and looked up to her, and they occasionally would sit in the Staff Room and chat about life, work, the past and the future. They got on very well. She loathed the other security guards with a passion as she didn't appreciate the way they teased and mocked him behind his back.

They scuttled off whenever they heard her footsteps echoing down the corridors. She could hear them of course and smirked with much delight at their cowardice. One day she had walked into the storeroom and had confronted one of them about how he had performed a shoddy piece of work when he should have carried it out in a far more efficient manner - like Bob. One scowl from her eyes had reduced the poor man to a gibbering stuttering wreck. She got off on this of course and the feeling of total control and power frequently produced a glow of pride in her heart that would be completely undetected by anyone else. But Bob had overheard sometimes, and his heart leapt within his chest on more than one occasion.

The man had tripped over some boxes on his way out of the room as the atmosphere in there had become so unbearable that he couldn't wait to get out of there fast enough! She had kept a straight face while glaring at him, but inside she guffawed uncontrollably and, did so audibly...when he was out of earshot. "Stupid incompetent bastard," she mumbled to herself, as she sorted out boxes of Patient Admittance forms, thousands of files and notes that had become too many to fit in the Main Office upstairs, on the first floor.

The boxes were covered in cobwebs and dust in the basement and, although she had a strict and grumpy nature, she was a wimp whenever she saw a creepy crawlie such as a spider that would run across a box over the top of her hand, making her shriek and squirm. Bob would hear her and would come to her 'rescue' many a time, and they would both have a good giggle about how she would be murdered by an insect if he hadn't been there.

Bob had a gentle nature, he would sit and observe the spiders when on duty, he marvelled at how delicate they looked yet how resilient they were. If one ever crawled across his hand he would merely lift his hand and look at it, unflinching, and, considering how big some of the spiders were, it was an admirable thing to do as none of his work colleagues would have the courage. They were all talk, all front, all pathetic - to him. They resented him because he worked with an efficiency and an honourable attitude that they could never maintain - they were envious and jealous.

He was oblivious to this and had long ago stopped fretting over the uncomfortable atmosphere between them all. He just resigned himself to the fact that they didn't like him, so he would just go about his work and get on with it, whilst ignoring them. Weeks ago he had teased them by warning them that he would set Matron upon them! A silly thing to do as they had thrown a chair at him, so he resisted the temptation to do that again! The bruise on his arm had taken days to fade and each time he examined it he would vow one day to get them back, a dish best served cold, he thought...and he had all the time in the world...

Upstairs, in the main office, Claudia concentrated and focused on some new Patient Admittance forms. Poring over each sentence, she copied the information onto the computer in front of her. She had learned to speed up with her typing and found that it enabled her to have extra time chatting with Bob downstairs when all the patients were asleep in their securely-locked rooms. She ensured each of them were sound asleep and sedated before she would go downstairs to the basement area, and there were never any problems.

It was a very old building, over 400 years old to be precise, and many patients had been treated there, looked after and, many had died there also... The walls were painted in a boring shade of grey, the paint peeled in the corners and the smell of disinfectant filled the air. Nobody could smell it anymore - as you get accustomed to a familiar aroma - on a daily basis. Only the patients families could ever smell it and some would sit in the Visitors Room holding their noses, screwing up their faces as they inhaled the unpleasant fragrance. Visiting times were strictly upheld; 2pm to 3pm and 7pm to 8pm daily, and she ensured that not one second would go overtime!

Patients were escorted to their rooms at 10 o'clock and then it was 'light's out' for sleep. The other nurses would walk up and down the corridors making sure that none of the patients were found half-asleep wandering around within their rooms; causing disturbance to the others, and if they were they were restrained in heavy-duty shackles...so they soon learned to behave accordingly.

Nurses also ensured that the rooms were maintained to a high standard of cleanliness and appearance; no urine-stained clothing was ever tolerated, for example. No sharp objects were to be found in any of the rooms so that none of the patients would harm themselves and, after visitors had left the building, each room and patient was searched thoroughly - just in case.

It was a very strict and depressing environment and the grey-painted walls just added to the dismal misery. One of the nurses had once offered to paint the walls a cheery yellow colour but had been reprimanded instantly. It had been her first day on the job and she had walked out after Claudia had shouted at her. Staff never seemed to last long there!

Bob wandered down one of the stone corridors in the basement area and whistled a merry tune as he took his time. His smart uniform and shined-up shoes looked good on him and he knew it. He took pride in his appearance every day and whenever a scuff on a shoe appeared he would buy a new pair straight away. Whenever a seam on his jacket would tear, rather than sew it and repair it he would request a new jacket. He strived to look his best at all times and besides...he had his lady to impress!

He was a handsome man; slicked-back black hair, soulful dark brown eyes, a neatly-trimmed moustache above a dazzling smile. Claudia stared at him sometimes and would fantasise about how the two of them would be together in a romantic setting. He caught her staring at him and smiling once and he blushed profusely, a grin had spread across his face as he had turned around, pretending that he hadn't noticed her. But she knew that he had.

It made his entire day whenever she spent even five minutes of her time with him, it meant a lot to him, and he'd whistle when alone due to his contented heart at the respect that she always bestowed upon him. He' often wonder if she fantasised about his muscular torso and how large his cock was. He also wondered about how she would look naked. He often fantasised about that; evident in how many times a week he'd accidentally bang his thumb when hammering a nail into a wall to repair something or other.

As he walked towards the end of one corridor, he noticed a rancid aroma filling his nostrils; much like the smell of death - a sickly-sweet putrid rotting stench. *Oh it's just a dead rat probably* he thought, and got a shovel and an old box to place the creature in. As he walked back towards the area, the smell had vanished. Standing there scratching his head, baffled, he looked around and shrugged his shoulders, resigning himself to the fact that he must be tired and had imagined it.

He placed the shovel and box back in the storeroom and walked back out, locking the door, the key jangling against lots of other keys that fitted different doors down the endless corridors of the creepy building. He had taken the labels off each key over the years as he knew by memory and feel which key fitted which lock. He had a photographic memory too, which helped enormously. As a very observant man, few details escaped his notice - a useful skill to have in an environment where monitoring safety was of paramount importance.

Protecting everyone in there was something that he took extremely seriously - unlike his colleagues - who loathed his efficiency due to the fact that it emphasised the lack of theirs. He was aware of how incompetent they were, but he kept his thoughts to himself for fear of being lynched and, the thought of their simmering resentment exhibiting itself on the end of their clenched fists wasn't something that he relished.

He wasn't afraid of them, he just preferred a quiet life on the whole and avoided confrontation at all costs. Claudia admired this about him as she was the same by nature - despite her fearsome reputation for taking no nonsense and her stern presence to anyone that didn't know the 'real' her; a shy and gentle soul at heart.

As Bob walked back up the corridor, he continued whistling and, behind him something...or someone had been watching his every single move. There was a noise coming from one of the corners; the creature slowly shuffled across the stone floor toward him... Bob didn't hear it as he jangled his large bunch of keys in his left hand, shaking them in tune to the song that he whistled loudly. He enjoyed music immensely and would repeat from memory all the rock songs that he could replicate.

The spirit behind him drew closer and closer, its icy cold fingers reached out and were inches away from his feet. It had hollow eyes and a snarling grimace on its face, its facial expression contorted into one of rage and anguish. Bob continued to stroll up the corridor. He took out his pocket watch and checked the time.

"Ah, Claudia will be here for a chat anytime soon" he muttered to himself, smiling. "She wont be long now Bobby boy!" He smiled broadly and his heart beat a little faster. The spirit behind him vanished through the wall as Matron's shoes echoed in the distance. She was approaching and Bob hurried up as the anticipation of seeing her again became unbearable. He couldn't wait one second longer. The spirit appeared again, lurking in the corner - watching and waiting...

"Bob, we need a wheelchair up in room three. Brenda's banged her leg on the radiator and she can't walk very far, she needs assistance to go to the canteen, for her dinner."

"Oh hi Claudia, I'll just get one for her from the storeroom. There's a wonky wheel on one of them which I'm repairing this week so I wont give you that one, you can have the new one that arrived last week, for her."

"You're *such* a darling, do you know that? I don't know *what* we would do without you here as you do *so* much more than is required from you, Bob!"

As they both walked into the storeroom and pushed the heavy steel wheelchair into the corridor, he felt her fingers brush his; it was only momentarily but the electricity that bolted up his arm and into his body, from her unexpected touch, sent sensations through him that he had never experienced before - he wanted more - but dared not ask. He felt a stirring in his cock but forced himself to focus on something else to think about.

"Mat...Matron, I um...” he said, coughing, “...I hope that you had a nice afternoon on Saturday at your sister's house."

"Oh I did, she took me shopping for new shoes and a handbag, we had *such* a blast!"

As she wittered on about her purchases, he fixated on her mouth; oh that smile, the way it lit up her face creating a spark within her sky-blue eyes. She was a very attractive woman, her teeth were perfect - he thought that everything about her was - perfect.

Oblivious to the spirit that stood behind them, they engaged in light-hearted conversation; mostly about the previous weekend's activities and what they would both do over the coming weekend. The spirit, a gentleman in his late fifties, had worked there decades ago, a deranged patient had suffocated him with a pillowcase while he had been crouching down upstairs in room four - repairing a broken radiator. She had crept up on him from behind and had silently slipped the pillowcase over his head, then had quickly twisted it around his neck as she pinned him down on the bed.

Despite his frantic thrashing about, he hadn't stood a chance. As his body slumped to the concrete floor, she had dragged him by the legs and had hidden his twitching body underneath her bed - where it lay all day - slowly decomposing. Matron had put the stench down to a rat that may have found its way upstairs from the basement and it took a week to work out that it was the corpse of Tom; who by then had filled up with bodily gases which had eventually leaked out from his swollen burst skin - much like a reddish-black sticky oozing jam - that had escaped from a large jar; too messy to even contemplate putting back in.

Paramedics took hours to scrape up what was left of him. The patient, Jean, had simply laughed when questioned as to her motive for killing him. No remorse registered within her empty eyes. Her response when asked by psychiatrists as to why she suffocated and then strangled him, was: "Because he took too long to fix the radiator and I was bored"...

The various nurses that worked in the asylum were of different ages and had differing abilities of efficiency; due to some having worked there for many years, to others having recently started after leaving University. There were ten in total: Penelope, Sophia, Michelle, Mary, Susan, Alison, Kerry, Olivia, Donna and Elizabeth. Numerous other nurses visited occasionally; to cover their holidays, sickness, and so forth.

~CHAPTER TWO~
The history of Mordithax asylum

The asylum; an old dismal-looking greyish-white building, had been built in 1714, upon Losgyth church. Next to the church lay a huge well-occupied cemetery; which had previously been blessed as a sacred area by Reverend Charlie Thomas, in the little village of Slayum Sanddownlea, in the town of Mordithax. It had previously spanned acres of woodland that had been removed to make way for the building that had been situated in the middle of it and, a few hundred villagers had inhabited the surrounding areas.

Menfolk would harvest crops and the women would tend to the home and the children. Animals would either be used as food or to pull carts that contained foodstuffs or clothing that had been produced in the nearby sister village of Cimonde - situated a few miles to the North. Slayum Sanddownlea had existed as a quiet town and, the townsfolk were inclined to have kept themselves to themselves; only speaking with fellow neighbours whenever they walked past each other or had combined their skills to create whatever the villages had required to consume, wear or had used for housing purposes.

Children were kept indoors and were taught at home - there were no public schools. Ancient in habits and twice as old in attitudes, the belief back then was that of a disturbed one; a curse had been placed upon the two villages by an elderly witch, that whomsoever walked near the church and discovered The Book - would be stone dead within 24 hours; unless they were a relative or friend; in which case they would be spared. The church, which was now the old asylum, had been demolished at the order of the police who went on to govern and uphold new laws - contrary to what the local Reverend had advised - that must at all times be adhered to, or else the consequences would be most dire.

The Reverend's mysterious disappearance was never discussed by anyone as they knew that the witch was probably responsible for it. The gossip was rife for many years. Since the building had been removed, life in the village had gone on peacefully - before the fire began, claiming their lives.

Reverend Charlie Thomas, the brother of the elderly witch, had ceased all communication with her due to her unconventional beliefs - which he had detested and, he felt embarrassed by her connection to him as a holy man. She had warned him on many an occasion that the church was haunted by the souls of those that he had preached to who had all festered a hatred toward him after discovering who he was related to. They saw him visiting her on more than one occasion in the past and had wrongly assumed that he was into devil-worship and the like. He had never engaged in such things of course, but nevertheless they didn't realize this.

The witch had also warned him that the surrounding land was haunted also, but her words had fallen upon deaf ears. She had gradually become cut off and ignored by anyone that had crossed her path. She had mysteriously disappeared - along with her brother and, the villagers had carried on with life as normal; ignoring the curse that she had placed upon the land. She had sent out the curse as the religious folk had slandered her repeatedly, reducing her to a miserable wretch of a woman and, over the years she had grown into a bitter angered soul.

Many years passed and the asylum had been built where the old church had once stood. The bodies beneath the graves of everyone that had died in the two villages throughout the years of; old age or natural causes, still remained, and were maintained by the local authorities. Two unmarked graves had been erected to remember Reverend Thomas and his elderly sister - old Haggetywren, the witch. Their bodies were never found. A stone plaque in the middle of the two graves had the inscription engraved upon it which read;

"The curse, the curse of old Haggetywren, placed upon all women and men, shall from henceforth be broken, the villagers have spoken. Venture out into the night-time, have no fear in the daytime, whomsoever passes this way, to you a safe and good day'! The curse is no more, it and the Witch have passeth away for sure!"

After the asylum had been erected and completed, things had taken a sinister turn. Electrics often played up and the plumbing system stopped working for months. The cause was never put down to an evil influence by the witch, it was thought to have just been 'one of those things' due to the ground settling or weather conditions. The surveyors, engineers and builders had believed in several reasons but they did wonder at the back of their minds if the problems were caused by something that they just couldn't bring themselves to speak to each other about.

As the months had passed by, patients were admitted into the asylum and were taken care of; day in, day out, and life became bearable. The gossip about the witch had subsided finally, and the villagers just got on with things as usual. Modern houses and apartments now replaced the old straw-covered cottages, and appliances and furniture worked efficiently, there was running water too!

But, down in the basement area, the electrics continued to play up - regardless of many electricians suggesting that it was the weather or other factors. Several staff members had received electrical shocks regularly; not enough to kill them but more than enough to frighten the living daylight's out of them from week to week.

Claudia had adjusted to it over the years to the point that it no longer bothered her, if anything she'd jest about it, and would often be heard saying "Ooooh I wont have to perm my hair with this lot going on in here!" she would just laugh it off, rather hoping that her jovial flippant attitude towards it would reassure others that if they did likewise then they would stop freaking out with constant anxiety. But she knew deep in her soul that the witchs' curse and all that she knew about her - she believed was true.

Reverend Charlie Thomas' friends had left documents for his family to read. One letter claimed that he had to go away to attend to family matters and that he would return as soon as possible - he never returned. His sister Jenny had tried for a while to get to the bottom of the matter but after her death of a sudden heart attack the remaining family let the matter rest. Nobody seemed to want to get involved and were scared witless to bother. They were reluctant to provoke attack from the witch, so they let the matter rest.

After much time had elapsed and, after the asylum had been completed, everyone had celebrated that the land was sacred again and the curse had been obliterated forever. Little did they know though that things were going to get a lot more interesting over the coming years and that some things never really go away at all...they just lie dormant for a while - and then erupt without warning.

The spirits of the churchgoers occasionally wandered through the corridors of the asylum, as if replaying their regular visits to Worship at the former church, they would emit anguished moans and tortuous sounds but workmen in the building often put it down to the old creaky pipes causing the din. Some patients that were being treated at the place were related to the spirits; who watched over them and protected them from the misunderstood witch. Their souls never rested. Now it was the year 2033 and the presence of those assumed long gone was very much still evident...

~CHAPTER THREE~
An unexpected visitor returns...

Bob sat down and rifled through his lunchbox for some delicious sandwiches - ham and cheese were today's selection - his favourite. He licked his lips in eagerness and savoured each morsel. Glancing around the canteen, he spotted his fellow work colleagues who sat on opposite sides of a table - precisely twenty feet away from him; far enough away from him to make it crystal-clear that his company wasn't sought. Their distance spoke volumes but he didn't allow it to get to him.

He put a radio on and enjoyed some music, turning the volume up to drown out the voices of gossip nearby. He had a very laid-back and calm attitude to life and never allowed others immature ways to rile him. In his job he had to remain clear-headed and relaxed at all times, and in doing so he carried out an exemplary work; apprehending many an intruder in the wee small hours - drug addicts who mistakenly thought it a good idea to sneak into the building searching for a quick fix - only to find themselves on the end of a rather large size 12 boot - and into a waiting police car.

One had pulled a knife on him a few years ago only to find Bob's adept skills in karate too much for them to challenge, and he had ran off like the coward that he was. The knife had landed on the stone floor, clattering as it did so. Bob being ever careful, had picked it up with a gloved hand, keeping the fingerprints on the handle as evidence for the police to use to capture the baddie. He had been praised many times by the police for his help and for risking his life in the face of potentially dangerous situations. One officer had even recommended that Bob join the force but he preferred his work at the asylum. Besides...he enjoyed the company of Claudia and would never leave her.

One of the patients upstairs had somehow managed to unlock her room door and began wandering down the corridor. Claudia sat in the main office sorting out the medicines and hospital restraints as a new patient was being admitted that day. She was oblivious to the patient around the corner who seemed delighted to have 'escaped'. She searched for the Fire Exit door but couldn't find one before one of the other patients began banging on her door to attract Claudia's attention. She ran out of the office, locking the door behind her as she did so and ran down the corridor to capture the woman. She walked her back to her room and scolded her.

"If I find you out of your room again young lady, you shall be detained in your room all the time, do you understand?"

"Yes Matron, it wont happen again, I promise!" had replied the sullen patient.

Claudia thanked the other patient for helping out and promised that she would give her an extra reward on the weekend as way of a thank-you - a new chair that she could throw - only Claudia smirked as the chair would be bolted to the floor, which would piss Brenda off enormously as she had a fondness of throwing chairs around at anyone that got in her way. The patient, Brenda, pulled a face at the other, Tricia, and stuck her tongue out, mocking her feeble escape attempt. She had done much better last month and had actually got past the Fire Exit door, had stumbled down the stairwell; before her capture by Bob, who was on his way up to collect his new uniform.

As the two women persisted in taunting each other, Claudia unlocked the office door and shook her head.

"Bloody kids, they're in their thirties yet they act like kids! I'm trying to get some bloody work done in here!"

She sat back down and took her shoes off her aching swollen feet. She must walk miles she thought to herself and the endless corridors did indeed seem just that some days

- endless. God knows how Bobs' poor feet must feel, he's on them all night and size 12's too! She rubbed her arches and toes and closed her eyes, sipping her coffee and sighing blissfully as the aching began to subside. The 80's music on the radio soothed her jangled nerves and reduced her stress dramatically.

She loved music and would sometimes dance in her black leather swivelling chair when nobody saw her, as she didn't want them to see her jovial side, only her strict bossy abrupt side, as it upheld the atmosphere of a disciplined environment - and kept the patients in line. They would never be capable of taking advantage of her good nature as she refused to stand for it. In her younger days as a nurse, she had been on the unfortunate end of that until experience had taught her to toughen up and to keep her wits about her at all times. Some of the patients; although mentally ill, knew exactly what they were doing and were manipulative and extremely clever. Many a time she had ducked as a chair had headed in her direction, narrowly missing her head - thrown by an impatient and irritated Brenda, who had yet another tantrum due to dinner not being on time - Tricia had walked in and informed her of this. Big mistake.

Bob made Claudia jump as the crackle from his walkie-talkie triggered off hers on the table in front of her. She sighed as she opened her tired eyes and put her shoes back on.

"Hi Bob, how are you today my dear?"

"I'm fine, Claudia, thank you, how are you? I just wanted to ask if you have my new jacket up there as this one has a tear in the elbow I'm afraid."

"Yes, it's here, ready and waiting for you, come on up to collect it, I can't leave the patients as it's not lights-out time yet, and my feet are killing me today!"

"Ok, I'll be up now in five minutes, if you're having a cuppa I'd love one too if that's alright, as I'm on my coffee break."

She told him that there was one waiting for him and some chocolate biscuits too. She placed the walkie-talkie back on the table and arranged the biscuits on a white bone china plate. She licked the melting chocolate from off her fingers and smiled.

"Mmm, I would love to kiss the chocolate off his lips!" she whispered to herself - but he had heard every word - as she had accidentally held her finger on the walkie-talkie button for too long... A broad grin spread across his face. It remained there for several minutes as he savoured her words that echoed in his mind.

As she sat there waiting, a ghostly hand touched her shoulder.

"That was quick, Bob, I thought you'd take longer than that!" She turned around to hand him the plate of biscuits and saw that nobody was there. Her eyes opened wide and she rubbed them; assuming that she were that tired that she was now imagining things. Bob knocked on the door out of respect for her - and protocol - and, noticing her startled expression he asked her what was wrong.

"You've gone as white as a sheet, what's the matter?"

"Well, I thought it was you just now, tapping my shoulder, but when I turned around to hand you these biscuits, there was nobody there." "I thought it must have been another member of staff but they couldn't have walked away in seconds like that, it's impossible. Maybe I'm overtired Bob and I imagined it, I can't be sure."

They both sat down and sipped their coffee and dunked the biscuits into the hot steaming delicious liquid. She handed him his new jacket and offered him a new pair of shoes too as he had had the other ones for months now and the soles must be on the way to being worn out - just as she felt that she was. He thanked her for the new jacket and put the shoes in a bag to keep in his locker downstairs in the basement. They listened to some music and turned the volume down as 10 o'clock approached for lights-out for the patients to get to sleep. He chatted to her about his busy day and she told him about hers. They got on very well together and always felt refreshed whenever they were in each others company.

As she turned off the lights for each of the patients rooms, she accompanied Bob downstairs to the basement area. He walked behind her and admired her silky black seamed tights. She sensed that he was looking at them. He loved the way her dark blue uniform accentuated her curvaceous waist, luscious bottom and hips and, although he was much taller than her, by looking down he could also see her cleavage; if he glanced over her shoulder. Tallness was a distinct advantage, he thought... She had a disciplined and bossy stride in her step and swung her arms back and forth rigidly, not allowing her shoulders to relax and to drop.

He often worried that her persistent neckache was down to this problem, but he daren't bring it up in conversation as he feared that she would reprimand him for commenting on her body, which, given half the chance he would worship all day. He had placed her on a pedestal for many years, and he would never do anything to offend or to embarrass her, so, mentioning her walking style would mortify him, especially if she gave him that stern look that she so often gave to others that they imagined would turn them to stone in an instant!

They reached the end of one of the basement corridors and peered around for any signs of; rats, intruders of a human kind or anything else unwelcome. There was nothing tonight, everything seemed fine. Back up the corridor they marched, this time chatting like the old friends that they were, her shoulder relaxing now and the stress disappearing from her previously furrowed brow. He too relaxed and consoled himself with the fact that even if he couldn't touch her, her warm company was more than enough for now. He masturbated at home some days after work, and cried soon afterwards; tears of loneliness, sadness at the agony of unrequited love, frustration. She would do the same, but they never confessed it to each other. Their deep friendship would be compromised and possibly ruined, they thought.

Then they would return to work as if everything was ok, but it was far from ok. They both engrossed themselves in their work and buried their feelings at the back of their minds. One day they would talk about it all, but there was too much to do in the asylum yet to find the time to sit down and have a detailed indepth conversation about matters of the heart. As Bob walked behind her, he felt something touch his leg. It made him jump and turn around instantly, in a split-second he reacted by reaching out and punching an unseen 'person', his hand swung around wildly into nothingness and Claudia screamed as an icy-cold hand crept around her warm neck.

They both stared into the contorted face of an anguished woman who screamed with an almost animalistic cry; one of pleading, begging, with a pitiful wretched expression filling her eyes. But they weren't hanging around for long to find out who she was or what she wanted! They both ran into the elevator and pressed all the buttons frantically. Ashen-faced and sweating profusely, their hearts pounded within their chest like a rhythmical banging of drums. It seemed like forever as each second dragged by as the elevator sluggishly climbed upward; the thick steel wires hoisted their metal room - or potential tomb - to the safety of Floor One. A screeching rang in their ears as the shrill screaming of the witch below them echoed for what seemed like an eternity.

~CHAPTER FOUR~
All is not well!

As they ran into the main office, they both slammed the door shut and looked at each other as they trembled uncontrollably. The colour had drained from their faces and perspiration dripped from off their bodies; they were terrified and had never experienced such fear in their entire lives. The temperature within the room plummeted and with each breath that they exhaled, they could see a hazy mist before them. A shuddering icy sensation ran up their spines and they steadied themselves by holding onto the large desk in front of them.

"What the hell was *that* down there!" Claudia whispered.

"Well I've been working here a long time and I've never seen anything like that before and, with all due respect, I'd like to take the rest of the week off!" said Bob, his eyes wide with petrifaction.

He wasn't his usual composed laid-back cheery self and the fear etched upon his face was too much for Claudia to bear so she agreed that one of his colleagues would stand in for him until he had recovered from his frightful experience. They agreed that they wouldn't tell anyone about it as if word got out, the Press would descend upon them all in an instant and the place would possibly be closed down. They weren't in a financial position to lose their jobs or to be relocated elsewhere due to the distance of the nearest asylum - which was 50 miles away.

After a slug of strong whiskey, they both sat and relaxed; their pulse rate had long since returned to a normal rhythm now and they both even found themselves giggling a little at what had occurred several hours ago. The other nurses that checked in on the patients had wondered why the office door had been locked and just assumed that she'd been having a private chat with Bob about work procedures or similar, so they busied themselves in their duties of; cleaning, caring, checking and monitoring every patient's room - and their whereabouts, and how they were today in general regarding medication and so forth.

The nurses wore the same bright white spotlessly-clean uniforms and strode around in black flat shoes upon the dark, grey, painted concrete floors. Claudia and Bob rubbed their heads and groaned as the effect of the alcohol subsided hours later.

"It's time for us to turn in for the night, Bob, we have an early start in the morning and lots to do."

"Yes Claudia, I'll be on my way soon, but it was wonderful as usual to relax and to enjoy our occasional meet-up for a good chat and to catch-up on events, and I hope that you are ok now after our little scare earlier?"

"Yes Bob, it's quite amusing now on reflection and it seems eons ago, not hours, we probably imagined it due to being so tired, I'm not sure if we hallucinated or what!"

She unlocked the door and bid Bob a goodnight as she smiled and grasped a set of keys from the top drawer of a filing cabinet. She wandered up the corridors to check that each door was securely-locked to prevent the unfortunate occurrence of a patient 'escaping' and hurting themselves by falling, or similar.

She also walked through the office doorway and began her routine check. She heard Bob softly humming to himself as he approached the elevator entrance to go to the basement, where he would sort his freshly-laundered uniform and other items for the following morning's workshift. Claudia smiled as she had always thought that he had a rather pleasant voice and mused that he should have taken up singing as a professional career, instead of a being a security guard at the asylum.

But she felt grateful that he chose to work with her instead, due to the deep fondness that she felt for him. She straightened her starch-white collar on her uniform and ruffled her hair as the hair lacquer that she had applied that morning was now making her neck itch; it irritated her skin something awful and so she scratched her neck furiously.

"Damned hair-spray!" she muttered.

As her black leather shoes squeaked down the corridor, she relished the sensation of her satin knickers caressing her inner thighs; like a kiss from a soft mouth, something that she hadn't felt in years - but longed for. Her mind often drifted to days and moments when she would frolic among the grassy fields with the farmer's son, George; a nice down-to-earth chap but too infantile in behaviour for her liking.

Claudia preferred her suitors to be rugged, masculine and up to her standard - bossy. She had not yet met her match, she had not yet been aligned with her 'other half', her soulmate, but she was sure that he was out there somewhere, if not in this life - he would exist in another. Bob filled her heart with unfathomable joy and delight, but she felt that he wasn't her soulmate...unless he proved otherwise as time ambled by.

~CHAPTER FIVE~
Revisiting the past...

Bob adjusted his shirt collar and whistled shrilly whilst standing in the elevator. He became aware of a presence near his left side and gulped nervously. As the floor indicator needle on the LED display seemed to take an eternity to count down, he noticed from his peripheral vision that a looming shadow began surrounding his body and, in a moment, he felt himself sink to the hard floor and drift into unconsciousness.

When he came to, he saw himself somewhere else; in a scene from what appeared to be another time, another century - nothing that he had ever seen in his own. Sitting up and scratching his head, he slowly regained his bearings and the sensation of disorientation subsided. As he stood up he saw in the distance a huge building that reminded him of something out of a fairytale story that his mother had conjured up as he had nightly drifted off to sleep. She was excellent at storytelling and he had a multitude of fond memories of that time.

As his vision adjusted and cleared, he could make out a large clock on what appeared to be a Town Hall white marble building. People were scurrying about their business; much like busy ants - everywhere looked bustling and very much alive. He was in a dream, he thought, and slapped his face to wake himself up.

The scene before him remained the same. "This can't be!" he said as he made his way across the hilltop down into the village square. His feet felt heavy upon the grass and he noticed that his clothing was vastly different; a black silver-sequined shirt, black boots, black trousers and a dickie-bow tie. He stared in disbelief at himself and shook his bewildered head. He was definitely in the throes of a dream he assumed and carried on walking towards the Town Hall.

He observed many women that were adorned in long flowing chiffon and satin gowns and ridiculously high-heeled shoes which they seemed to be attempting to look elegant upon but one tottered then regained her balance; glancing around embarrassed, just in case anyone else had noticed. He had...

He was struck by her beauty, black flowing locks of wavy hair cascaded down her back and she had the kind of curvaceous body that would mesmerise any red-blooded man.

"Alice, there you are!" she cried, as she smiled and stretched out her arms, embracing the other woman affectionately. They hugged and scuttled off into the Town Hall. There was a lot of commotion going on, a party atmosphere, and he wanted to walk in there with the two women but he thought it wise to lie low; so as not to be noticed.

As he approached the huge ominous-looking stone building with its white marble pillars and deep engravings - taking his breath away with their impressiveness, he noticed quite a lot of sculptures that depicted animal gods and religious symbols; they towered over him much like enormous creatures from another world - and he felt so small and insignificant in comparison.

As he strolled into the building, he sat at the far back, by the door, trying to appear inconspicuous, but the attractive lady and her friend noticed him instantly.

"Hello Charlie, it's so nice to see you again, come and sit by us this instant!"

He looked behind him as he felt they were addressing someone else but, there was no-one else behind him, they were talking to him!

"Hello, I'm sure that you have me mistaken for someone else, but it's nice to meet you likewise." Who *is* this Charlie? he wondered.

"Charlie, come and sit beside us, stop talking nonsense!" the two women insisted.

He thought them to be quite mistaken - or quite mad, so he walked over to them; confused but elated that he could sit by the dark-haired beauty that had so caught his eye previously and with whom he was completely smitten and enthralled by. He whispered to her that his name wasn't Charlie, it was Bob, but she laughed; looking at him oddly.

Her hand touched his and she nudged her hips right up next to his as she glanced around the room. Who is this woman? he mused to himself, but he didn't care, he was mesmerised by her, and words didn't really matter - as she obviously liked him. Her friend chatted to her about the day, life, all sorts, and they were oblivious to his curiosity about them, how they knew him and who they were.

He still felt that he were dreaming the incident and just let it all wash over him and that he should simply go with the flow of it all. He would wake up soon, he assured himself, so he sat there quite happily - but blissfully unaware of a dark presence that hovered behind him... The hairs on the back of Bob's neck stood bolt upright but he put the sensation down to a draught as the Town Hall's door lay wide open.

A red-haired woman walked in; her blindingly-white dress wafted past the audience, toward the altar. She oozed serenity and calm and her eyes were fixated upon a gentleman - looking rather dapper at the far side of the aisle - waiting for her hand to fit into his, like a glove.

The general mood in the atmosphere was that of joy and excitement. This was a wedding! He noticed that it wasn't a Town Hall, but rather it was a very large church that had been built upon a Town Hall. He peered around the room and, to his horror and surprise, he recognised everyone that sat there. "This must be one of those weird vivid dreams," he whispered to himself; shaking his head to wake his senses, but there he remained.

He felt a cold grip on his shoulder and his heart almost stopped with the fright of it all. As he slowly turned his head to see exactly who sat behind him, the dark-haired companion sitting beside him gripped his other wrist, but that felt warm and friendly.

"So Charlie, what do you think of Victoria and Tim getting married then?" I bet you never thought you'd see *those* two ending up together; especially as she did the dirty on you years ago, leading you on for all those years and then vowing never to marry you, and Tim doing exactly the same to me!" "But, forgive and forget eh!"

Bob looked at her and told her that he needed to get outside to gather his thoughts and to grab a breath of fresh air, as he felt dizzy.

The woman's friend called her name, gesturing for her to go outside with her to have a cigarette.

"Becky, let's sneak outside for a quick cigarette, we can always sneak back in halfway through the ceremony and they wont even notice that we've gone!"

As the three of them walked outside, Bob mulled over her name in his mind. Becky, Becky, *Becky* - what a nice-sounding name. He smiled and stood by the entrance. In his breast pocket he felt the outline of a pipe and proceeded to light the tobacco in it with a match from a box that he had stuffed into the back pocket of his trousers. As he leaned against the doorframe watching the two women puffing on a cigarette, he noticed that Becky had a bruise on her forearm.

"So, how exactly do we know each other, as I'm a little muddled?" he asked them both.

"Charlie, what are you on today, you are not your usual self, you've known us since we were children, your brother is the priest who is conducting the wedding of our friends!"

"I last recall being in an asylum as a security guard, that's all I know, yet I come down here and I recognise you all, so if I'm dreaming, pinch me!"

The two women pinched him and he yelped in pain, he wasn't dreaming as in his usual dreams he didn't normally feel any pain registering in his body, but if this was a dream, that hurt...a lot!

"What do you mean when you say that the priest is my brother?" "Who are our parents?"

"Oh they passed away many years ago, but your sister is still around." "After this wedding you can go and visit her if you like, she lives in the old wooden house; half a mile away from here, but she is avoided - nobody in this town bothers with her as she's not the kind of person anyone would want to associate with, well not after what she did to your brother..."

"What do you *mean*?" he inquired; a frown etched his brow.

"Well go and speak to her and she will fill you in on all the details I'm sure." "I thought that you already knew all of this, have you knocked your head today or something Charlie, as that memory of yours is usually so sharp, it's like you have have amnesia today or something!" she said, as she rolled her eyes and shrugged her shoulders; dismissing the confusion in a second.

Becky sauntered back into the wedding ceremony, along with her friend, Alice, and Bob stood outside pondering on the information that he had just been given. He silently willed himself to wake up but not really wanting to as Becky was so sublime and, if this *was* a dream, who knows if he would have the same one ever again. His heart was for Claudia but as she seemed to be taking her time over the years in declaring her undying love for him verbally, he saw no harm in showing affection to other women; after all, he was a man - and men have needs.

The wedding ceremony seemed to drag on endlessly as Bob gathered his thoughts by the doorway, so, he decided to venture back in; mainly out of respect for the proceedings - as he was an old-fashioned man and had always viewed marriage as a holy ceremony and a situation that one would find oneself in only if they truly loved another from the soul - as he did for Claudia. As he walked back into the room, he spotted a dark shadow crawling across the floor, unseen by others as nobody seemed startled or perturbed by it at all.

It was if he was the only person that could see it - and he was. He came to the conclusion that he was fatigued and sat back down near Becky who was now twirling one of her dark curls around her index finger, gazing at him from out of the corner of her long-lashed gorgeous blue eyes. Her make-up was perfection itself and she positively glowed with zest of life and a youthful inner joy. She smiled at him and he reciprocated. Her friend seemed quite the introverted and shy type, quieter than Becky, but equally as ravishing to his eyes.

The Ghostly Asylum of Mordithax

"I now pronounce you man and wife!" boomed the priest as the audience applauded - and some whistled in appreciation and approval.

Bob noticed when the groom turned around that he had glanced at him and that his jaw had dropped in a way that exhibited a guilty expression. Bob stared at the man but the man refused to maintain eye contact and hurriedly escorted his bride up the aisle and out of the building toward a waiting horse-drawn brightly ribbon-covered carriage. Bells chimed loudly and a procession of excited partygoers flocked around the vehicle; poised to throw rice over the newly-married pair. Bob didn't have any rice so he slowly made his way unnoticed through the cheering crowd and up the lane towards the old wooden house that his so-called sister resided within.

What would unfold, he wondered, and, what exactly would he find out?... Becky watched him and smiled as she knew he would indeed find the truth and would make sense of things that were obviously puzzling him. She sent three male friends to discreetly follow him to ensure his safety - as she already knew what was in store for him - as she had visited the witch on a previous occasion herself - hence the bruise on her arm, which was a painful reminder not to revisit her in future!

As Bob walked up the pathway and across a field full of stinging nettles and long-forgotten bound tree stumps, his heart raced as a trickle of perspiration dribbled down his clammy forehead. He wiped it away with a white cotton handkerchief and told himself to be courageous as his jangled nerves were trying their best to overcome his otherwise usual calm nature.

Several cats huddled together by a tree and played in the sunshine which shimmered across their shiny fur like diamonds bouncing off tiny strands of steel. One cat approached him and rubbed itself against one of his legs. "Puss puss, pssss." He softly spoke to the little creature affectionately as he had always been an animal-lover and would never do another being harm.

A face peered at him from one of the dusty windows; half obscured by dingy-looking net curtains. The house looked derelict and unkempt; much like its inhabitant.

What he saw was a vision of ugliness beyond the extreme and it was the face of a person who appeared to seriously neglect themselves; a disfigured, hideous wretch! Smoke filled his nostrils as the chimney spouted black thickness as dark as that of night. The fragrance of herbs filled the atmosphere and old dilapidated cars and trucks littered the yard; long ago used - judging by the amount of thick cobwebs that clung upon each corner and crevice. He stumbled upon a twig protruding from the undergrowth and although attempting to prevent himself from falling, he knocked his head on one of the tree stumps.

"Bob, did you fall and bang your head in the elevator?" cried a startled Claudia. He was somehow back in the asylum as she tended to his head wound, cradling him in her hands and on her lap.

"I'll be right back, I'm just going to get the First Aid kit, you need that wound cleaned and dressed straight away."

As Bob lay there on the elevator floor, he looked up and saw the remnants of a scrawny-looking twig that had become tangled up in his hair. Along with it were several black whiskers from that of a cat. He brushed them off him and slowly pulled the twig from the strands of his matted hair. He heard an eerie cackling laugh that came from the far end of the corridor and he shuddered as goosebumps ran across his trembling body.

Claudia returned promptly and tended to his bruised head. She kindly gave him the day off while the other security guards covered his shift.

~CHAPTER SIX~
An attempted escape!

The ten women that were confined within separate rooms were prescribed a variety of medications. Some of the women were: psychotic, some neurotic, some delusional, some paranoid, but all were aggressive - especially at unexpected moments - hence the strict level of security upon that floor of the asylum. Each of them were detained within their rooms for the majority of the time, and, if necessary, were restrained and sedated whenever violent tendencies arose; which were frequent but less in severity than they were in previous months. Brenda had the unfortunate habit of throwing chairs and random objects at Claudia whenever the opportunity arose. She, however, was used to this and simply ducked, which frustrated Brenda enormously!

She'd attempt to calm her down and would sit with her, but would always smirk when walking out of the room - as walking out unscathed and unhurt was a triumph of the day, she thought. A victory! Sheila suffered with paranoia and, assumed inaccurately, that everyone was out to 'get' her or were talking about her behind her back. Claudia discussed her behaviour with Dr Evans, the psychiatrist, on a weekly basis, but other than that nobody really paid Sheila any attention whatsoever.

Mildred was psychotic and neurotic and had random urges to hurt others; getting much glee and satisfaction from it when she used to exhibit this behaviour a lot more, in the past. But not now, as the relevant medication sorted that out once and for all and Claudia ensured that she never missed a dose; just to be on the safe side!

Janet often talked to herself and had imaginary 'friends' that she 'confided' in with her deepest darkest secrets...not realizing that every word uttered in each room was recorded anyway and, was relayed to the main office where Claudia listened intently while on her coffee and lunch breaks - when the nurses were on their rounds to check that all of the patients were in their rooms - not wandering down the corridors where they could harm others - or themselves.

Joanne was diagnosed with depression, fits of anger, violent mood swings and delusions of grandeur; not having the ability to get on with anybody left her sad and alone as others steered well clear of her very obvious irritating and unstable mood swings. Why her husband put up with her behaviour in the past was difficult to understand although...he was bordering on similar conditions himself on occasion.

Tricia was diagnosed with depression and severe paranoia. She was often found rocking back and forth on her bed; she was virtually impossible to console, but, she had an extremely intelligent mind and an untapped creative potential - which Claudia tried to coax out of her by providing her with art lessons, whenever the opportunity arose.

Jean was the most secretive and untrustworthy out of all the women and, was not one to be around on the weeks when she suffered from pms, because, although she was mostly silent and anti-social, she would often manipulate the other women to get her own way - a control freak. Her fits of anger combined with manipulative tendencies were her ultimate downfall.

Careen lived in her own fantasy world and would only come out of her shell whenever anyone paid her the slightest bit of attention; which she'd play upon in order to attempt to control them for her own gain in whatever ways satisfied her whims.

Nicola was the most aggressive of the women, frequently found punching walls and, on one occasion in the past, her fist had made painful contact with another patient's stomach. She was now in strict isolation and was never let out by herself, not even for one second; unless a nurse accompanied her, but not until Nicola had been cuffed.

Then there was Jessica. A habitual liar and untrustworthy sort, not to be trusted - not even for a moment. She suffered, or rather, enjoyed, masochistic tendencies and, created situations that would result in her being punished - often - as she enjoyed being reprimanded. She would get off on this - much to the Nurse's bemusement and, *no* amount of counselling from Dr Evans could do any good.

As Claudia checked on each of the patient's rooms, she noticed that Tricia wasn't in hers.

"Tricia, are you in the bathroom?" There was no reply. She walked towards the area, which was at the very end of the corridor and, she checked the cubicles, one by one; they were empty. She must be in the canteen or library Claudia thought, so, she made her way to both in that order. Tricia wasn't in either, so, the security guards were summoned to patrol the outside of the building as well as to explore inside too - until they found her.

Claudia marched off to speak to the nurses, and not one of them had seen any sign of

Tricia for at least two hours. They assumed that she had gone to her weekly art class, so, they went to check. The door was locked. Just then, one of the security guards, Adam, informed them all that he had found the patient huddled downstairs in one of the storerooms, busily sketching in an art book. She was so quiet that they hadn't even heard her footsteps on the hard stone floors and they weren't really doing their jobs as they had all been playing card games downstairs, instead of patrolling the corridors, as they were expected to.

"Nobody say a word about this, got it!" whispered Adam to the other guards, as he glared at them. They all nodded in unison and thought it wise to keep quiet about the situation.

Tricia was escorted back to her room and promptly given a check-up by one of the nurses to make sure that she hadn't harmed herself. She was fine.

"Please don't wander off again Tricia, we were *very* concerned about you dear!" said Donna, one of the nurses; a lady with a gentle disposition who also possessed nerves of steel as one was required in that job, due to the erratic behaviour of some of the patients. They had to be alert and to keep their wits about them at all times. When the nurse had consoled her, she sat beside her and attempted conversation; which was difficult at the best of times and, if she couldn't get her to open up then it was even harder for the other nurses to achieve success.

"Did you enjoy your little wander, my dear?" she gently inquired. She tidied Tricia's hair and moved it away from her face in a motherly gesture. Tricia nodded and continued looking down towards the floor. She whispered. The nurse didn't quite hear her so she sat closer and asked her to repeat whatever it was. The woman looked at her and directly stared into her eyes.

"When I was downstairs in the storeroom, I *wasn't* alone you know!"

Donna tried to conceal her building concern and calmly asked;

"What do you mean my dear, *who* was with you?"

"An old woman with eyes like burning fiery coals, and a face that was twisted in a hideous scary way!" "I saw her you know, I really *did* see her and she didn't do me any harm, she kept me company and told me all about her life and about the history of this place."

Nurse told her that she believed her - mainly to get her to go to sleep so that she could have some peace and then take her coffee break, but she doubted her story immediately; considering it as fantasy, poppycock and rubbish.

She assured the woman that she would return the next day and they could chat some more about it if it made her feel better. The door was locked and the lights were switched off; albeit for just the main one that dimly lit the corridor and it reassured the patients that they weren't completely in darkness.

Nurse Donna Thomas checked on the other women, then briskly made her way to the canteen for her well-deserved cup of coffee and cigarette. Some of the other nurses accompanied her and, she told them everything that Tricia had described. Some laughed and mocked, some changed the subject; as stories about witches and ghoulies sent shivers up their spines - they preferred instead - to discuss more 'pleasant' matters.

Claudia listened outside the door and crept away quietly on tip-toe so as not to be detected. She sat in the main office and sipped her tea - with a little whiskey added; a nightly treat that nobody knew about - except Bob. One wont do any harm she convinced herself, putting the bottle back into the filing cabinet drawer, then locking it via a combination lock.

Combing her hair she glanced out of the window at the forecourt below, watching some of the security guards as they patrolled the area in their smart uniforms and shiny black shoes. How smart and polished they all look, she thought. She wondered how Bob was and telephoned downstairs. He informed her that he was feeling much better after his fright, and he would be there in the next five minutes...for their usual evening chat - and whiskey! He was so grateful that she seemed to miss him when he wasn't around and, hearing her voice on the line brought back the smile upon his face.

~CHAPTER SEVEN~
Who goes there?

The next morning, rays of golden light shimmered through the curtains as the sun cast its glory upon the building. Visitors scurried to the elevator, which would take them to the rooms of their loved-ones upstairs; who waited for their arrival in the visitors lounge. All of the nurses busied themselves nearby as Claudia went on her usual morning checking routine; ensuring that all was as it should be in the building; regarding medication allowances and, precisely which one would be dispensed that day according to how each patient had responded previously to any other that had been administered to them.

All of them were monitored closely and there were never any accidents or cock-ups in the asylum as Claudia prided herself on impeccable service, health and that every single safety procedure was followed - to the letter, every little detail was scrutinised and triple-checked for accuracy and so forth.

Staff in the canteen clattered their pans and pots while scrubbing them to within and inch of their lives and they wiped up the residual droplets of porridge and yoghurt that had been either thrown, dropped or dripped onto the floor and counters by the medical staff and patients alike; some people have such sloppy manners they thought and would gossip about everyone behind their back as they busied themselves in their cleaning duties after everyone had left the room.

Head cook Mable wore a pristine-clean white uniform and hat, and there wasn't a ladder in her immaculately-smooth tights. She always had swept-back short hair and took no nonsense from anyone - least of all from her cooking staff who were beneath her in rank. If one of the staff got out of line, she would reel them back in sharpish and thought nothing of sacking them and swiftly replacing them - if necessary!

She had a reputation to uphold and it would *never* be allowed to falter! Bob usually sat in there by himself; timing it so that he wouldn't be in the tedious company of his fellow workmates whom he detested - due to their incessant psychological bullying. They were grateful for this gesture of course, as they couldn't stand him either! Many a time he had been tempted to hurl not abuse at them - but some rather lumpy thick custard their way, but he resisted the urge. It *did* amuse him nevertheless, to fantasise about this whenever he tucked into his boiled egg on toast.

Mable wiped the last of the tables clean and looked around the room for the remotest sign of untidiness and if even one crumb remained. Anything else would be completely unacceptable to her; according to her supremely-high standards of cleanliness, and how she viewed order. If everything was clean in her workplace then her life was less stressful and she could go home content. When she got home however, there was more work; cooking and cleaning.

She was always the last member of staff in the canteen to leave; locking the door behind her - mainly to prevent the unfortunate potential tragedy of a wandering patient getting their hands upon the sharp knives! She entered the security code into the alarm system, then locked the door, checking twice.

The floor sparkled, the countertops gleamed, the heat from the hot-washed cutlery rose off it in the drawers and came out of the gaps on the sides, like puffs of smoke. A fragrance of pine filled the air and would escape through the gap at the bottom of the door; filling the adjoining library with its fresh-smelling odour - much to the distraction of Claudia who was searching for a book on how to please a man in bed.

Passion and pine do not mix whatsoever, she thought, as she climbed up the library ladder, put on her reading glasses - which perched upon the bridge of her nose that had the annoying habit of slipping downwards as she glanced down at each book title.

The ladder began moving as she engrossed herself in reading one of the books from the erotic section, grinning broadly as her eyes found some rather explicit paragraphs. She continued reading, with much glee. The ladder moved again, this time very noticeably, startling her to the point that almost lost her balance and fell off. "This damn floor has been polished way *too* much today!" she muttered, cursing the cleaners. Several books suddenly fell off one of the shelves and the light went out. She carefully and gingerly climbed down the ladder, feeling the ball of her feet upon the rungs until she slowly reached the floor.

As she tried switching the light on in the creepy darkness, she realized that it already *was* turned on... The ladder moved again; creating a squeaky sound as it did so.

"Who goes there!?" she demanded. "Bob, is that you, messing around?"

Silence cut through the air like a samurai sword. The mood was one of eerie expectation. She could feel the hairs on the back of her neck stand bolt upright and her heart began to pound.

"Don't panic, keep calm!" she reassured herself; a tactic that she hoped would settle her nerves somewhat. A freezing-cold chill - much like that of the wall of coldness that encompasses the face after a refrigerator door is opened - engulfed her, causing her to shiver uncontrollably. She sensed that she wasn't alone, despite her rational mind desperately trying to convince her otherwise. Bob knocked on the door and shouted to see if she was in the room.

"Oh thank God!" "Bob, get me out of here *now*!" she screamed, relieved beyond words that his timing was *perfect* at that very moment. With anxious eyes, he rushed up to her and cradled her in his arms as the sight of her trembling with fear brought out his caring side for her.

He apologised profusely at his breach of protocol but, she ran out of the room with him, thanking him repeatedly; for rescuing her. They went to the main office and she barricaded the door - after locking it, with; a chair, a table and several boxes! As she gradually calmed down, she opened the whiskey bottle and gulped a mouthful before she could compose herself enough to sound coherent, to make sense.

"Bob, *I know* it wasn't my imagination, I felt someone was in that room with me, I *wasn't* imagining it *this* time!"

Relieved, he looked at her and told her about *his* experience: when he had banged his head in the elevator, only to instantly find himself in another time, a time where he believed he had lived before - in the past, a time where he knew everyone that had lived in the town that had thrived - before the asylum was built.

He explained to her that the witch that he had had a glimpse of for a mere second, was someone that he had known in a previous life, someone that would haunt and would follow him wherever he went; for a reason that would become clearer as time passed by. He told her that he had a sweetheart in a parallel lifetime, that he desired, and that she reminded him of her; which tugged at his heartstrings, someone that he was instantly drawn to and was attracted to - like a moth to an alluring hypnotic flame.

Could Claudia be that young woman that he had met? he wondered. She looked at him and shook her head, disputing his belief. She didn't believe in such things as parallel universes or lives, or in the paranormal, she was a rationally-thinking intelligent human being and prided herself on perceiving things from a scientific point of view - as opposed to that of a mere whim or a fancy.

He looked to the floor in utter disappointment, a painful sensation; like a jagged sharp knife, tore through his heart, at that very second. She reduced him to the deepest anguish imaginable. They changed the subject rapidly. They drained the bottle of whiskey dry and then bid their farewells for the evening. Bob dragged his heels on the floor, as he left her, and his body felt as heavy as lead - as did his heart.

Something *else* dragged itself behind him...

A murder of crows crowed; shattering the deafening silence with their eerie screams. The trees outside the asylum creaked with every angle that they sought to reach. The moon cast a spooky glowing curtain across the skies. All was silent in the building; for now. The patients sat in their rooms quietly, watching television.

Claudia splayed herself upon the carpet in the main office, picking up fragments of paper and paperclips, as the cleaning lady had called in sick for the day. While upon the floor, she stretched her arm and hand into a crevice underneath the filing cabinet to discover a screwed-up bunch of files in an old folder. She dragged it toward her face, sat bolt upright and began reading in earnest.

CASE FILE 304: Patient Thomas.

D.O.B: Unknown; awaiting update from family.

DIAGNOSIS: Severe psychotic episodes, delusions of grandeur, paranoia.

TREATMENT: Permanent confinement due to husband's inability to care for her at home.

Matron perused the file, word for word, carefully and thoroughly; her reading glasses perched themselves precariously upon the bridge of her sweaty nose. Her eyes scanned downwards and they fell upon a sentence that would shock her to her very core; 'Patient Thomas - wife of Mr Robert Thomas... She hid the document and thought it best that she studied it later after her workshift had ended.

On her rounds she couldn't get anything out of her mind apart from what she had read. Could this patient really be the wife of my Bob? she thought. As she walked past each room that the patients were confined in, she saw a notice upon each of the doors that the nurses had left for her:

'Matron, all of us have gone out for the day in a minibus, to Mordithax Flower Show. We'll be back later.'

"The fuckers!" "Hmm, why wasn't I asked permission about this, in advance!" she growled under her breath, as she gritted her teeth; seething that she hadn't been respected enough to have warranted at the very least a conversation with nursing staff. She stormed out of the building, black tights causing hot friction on her plump thighs underneath her crisp streamlined uniform. Her thighs chafed and burned with each stride that she took, but the venom within her spirit spurred her on, they were in for it now, she thought, for daring to over-ride her wishes, as no patient was *ever* allowed outside without *her* say-so!

She contacted them by telephone, they told her that they were waiting outside by the entrance. She marched outside and told everyone off sternly, then summoned them back inside for a lecture; demonstrating the correct respectful attitude towards her authority - *then* they were allowed to go to the Flower Show - on condition that a minimum of two of the nurses stayed behind, just in case their medical skills were needed in the asylum if she or the canteen staff required them.

She went back to the main office to read more about patient case files in privacy; there were important details that didn't seem to match, there were a number of errors that she had to get to the bottom of, and *soon!*

~CHAPTER EIGHT~
A portal to another world is discovered!

The elevators were playing up that day. Up was down, down was up. The emergency button had been pressed repeatedly by unseen fingers - much to the annoyance of the engineer who didn't have a moment of peace because of it.

"What the *fuck* is going on with this damn elevator today?" he ranted.

Claudia rolled her eyes and walked away.

"Just *fix* it please as the sound of that alarm going off every two minutes is driving me nuts!" "I can't bloody hear myself think, *and* I have work to do as well you know!"

The engineer battled for hours to stop the deafening din but alas to no avail; he just couldn't stop it from repeatedly going off. He dismantled it altogether.

"*Now* go off, you piece of shit!" he sneered.

The elevator began moving upward...and upward...and it didn't stop until it moved between two floors. The doors opened and, what greeted him was the horrific sight of a snarling, grimacing - face! He screamed. Then there was silence.

Claudia rushed up the stairwell and shouted for Bob and some of the other security guards to follow behind her. They pulled out the guns from their holsters and raced to the top floor. She ran back down; passing them on the way, her face devoid of any colour. The armed men crouched down as they crept slowly towards the elevator doors; gesturing to each other exactly when to shoot - if necessary. They stood in unison and shouted:

"Put your hands on your head, *right now*!"

They looked into the elevator, to find it - empty...

"There are some bizarre things happening in this building guys, some of you stand guard here, while I go onto a different floor." "I'll contact you on the walkie-talkie if I find the bastard."

Bob walked into the elevator and pressed the relevant buttons that would transport him to each of the floors, one by one. Downstairs, some of the guards were positioned with guns in hand, waiting... They waited some more; the anticipation became agonising. The elevator door slowly opened...it was empty.

"Bob must have got out on one of the other floors, guys, let's contact him to find out what the hell is happening!" The walkie-talkie crackled and the guards repeatedly called him. There was no response.

The engineer opened his eyes to find himself in unknown territory. He peered around and attempted to get his bearings; feeling *very* disorientated. He didn't recognise the buildings or the swarm of people that surrounded him.

"Where am I?" "Who *are* you all?" he asked.

"Well hello there!" "Are you feeling alright?" "You seem to have banged your head. Which town are you from as we haven't seen you around here before?"

He informed them that he had last recalled trying to repair an elevator in Mordithax asylum but, they assumed that he had concussion as they had never *heard* of such a place. They took him to the local surgery for a check-over and there was only one person that he *did* recognise - it was Dr Evans.

"Where am I, Doc?"

Doctor Evans explained to him that only he knew of a portal, a doorway, that existed between this place and Mordithax - and that they were one and the same place.

The engineer; Matthew, didn't believe him. *He must be dreaming*, he thought, *surely...*? Doctor Evans pulled out a huge dusty old book that he had discovered hidden underneath the church - under the thick, dusty, floorboards. Ravenous rats had done their best to eat away at the spine and the tough binding of the book but, most of the pages inside were relatively intact; albeit for several tiny teeth marks at the edges.

Written within this book were highly-detailed descriptions of parallel worlds and time travel. Detailed, colourful, illustrations, had been hand-drawn - depicting various hideous images. He had been studying it for many years and it was kept under lock and key, where only *he* had access to it. It spoke of a mysterious fantastic future where the old church was to be demolished and replaced with an enormous white stone building - an asylum for the mentally-disturbed. Built within the premises would be a portal; an invisible - but very real - doorway, to another world. A curse had been put upon this section of the asylum - by a witch. The book was signed by a Reverend C Thomas...

Matthew shook his head in disbelief at the revelation and refused to believe it. Dr Evans assured him that it was no joke and that it *was* indeed true. Besides, how else could he explain where he was now? He pinched him hard, to prove it.

"You don't feel *this* amount of pain when in a dream, Matthew!"

The man yelped and nodded in agreement as he rubbed sore skin. The Doctor made him a cup of coffee and checked him over to make sure there were no cuts or bruising. He seemed fine, so he gave him a clean bill of health. They sat and chatted about the town and the rapport between them improved. Maybe they could become good friends, but Matthew was desperate to get back to the asylum. But how could he? If this wasn't a dream then where was the portal doorway *now,* that would allow him access and transportation back into the future?

Dr Evans proceeded to explain and, to convince him, that if there is a way into this time and world - then likewise...there most definitely was a way *back* and, he would do his best to assist him. They walked around the town and chatted at length about; life, the future, the past and, all that lay inbetween it.

"Fancy a slug of whiskey in that coffee, Matthew, as you sure look like you need it and I always keep a hip flask handy just in case *I* need it, which, on a Monday morning, it's the perfect remedy for the *both* of us?!"

They sipped their cups of hot whiskey/coffee and had a good laugh about everything as they continued strolling around the area. While distracted from chatting, Dr Evans had forgotten to lock The Book back up. Icy-cold greyish-white fingers were busy removing it - and were hiding it elsewhere...

Meanwhile, back in the asylum, Claudia busied herself by chatting with Mable in the canteen. Mable had always disliked her, but had never let on, even concealing her contempt for her by altering her body language and mannerisms so that she wouldn't detect her dislike of her.

She was completely oblivious of this fact and would often sit at one of the tables chatting away during her morning coffee break.

As all of the patients had gone out for the day to the Flower Show, she had all the time in the world to engage others who were there; in idle chit-chat, to her heart's content. Mable tolerated this intrusion by nodding and smiling at the appropriate moments during the 'discussion' - as she simply *couldn't* get a word in - due to Claudia's relentless ramblings. She had never told anyone, that every night she would have the most *awful* recurring nightmares of violently attacking Claudia, but, she didn't have a clue as to *why*. After all, she couldn't possibly tell her about her dreams as she would have her sectioned under the Mental Health Act immediately! So, she kept silent about it and kept her thoughts to herself only.

"Mable, we *must* have lasagne on the menu soon, I adore that, especially when it's home-made - not that god awful microwaveable 'plastic' slop that poorly masquerades as lasagne from the supermarkets, ugh!"

Mable nodded, smiled, turned around and mouthed a silent 'ewww, *gross*!' Muttering obscenities under her breath, she poured Claudia another coffee; wishing it were arsenic-laced but, she resisted the urge to wet herself laughing at her 'evil' thoughts.

"Here you are, enjoy!"

She thanked her and sipped the coffee; dunking a chocolate biscuit into the steaming-hot liquid - half of it breaking off and sinking slowly to the bottom of the mug, before ending up on the top of the surface; much like a biscuity liferaft devoid of passengers.

"Oh bugger!" she said, continuing to gaze out of the nearby window. She liked sitting by the window as it overlooked the large rose-filled garden. Rays of intensely-beautiful sunshine danced upon each petal; causing the vibrant colours to appear luminous, glowing almost. 'Ahhh this is *soooo* nice,' she whispered to herself as Mable sorted out the menu for that week; scribbling out spaghetti bolognese and replacing it with lasagne - as she ground her teeth with frustration.

"I fucking *loathe* lasagne!" she hissed - out of earshot of Matron who, by now, was totally engrossed in observing a Red Admiral butterfly - engaging in dainty flight with another.

Dr Evans and Matthew returned to the surgery. Upon seeing that The Book had disappeared, they both began to panic as the implications and consequences that this would have for Matthew were too dreadful to contemplate, but, they *had* to find a way to get him back into the future - to the asylum. People would miss him and he would miss them, unbearably.

They ran to the edge of the church that had eventually been demolished to make way for the asylum in the future. Dr Evans knew of only one person that would steal The Book and he knew that she would return it to its original place; as nobody else would think to look there - except him. They grasped two shovels from the old ramshackle shed by the side of the building and, began to dig, and dig...and dig. Under the floorboards, they found nothing.

"It's *got* to be here!" said the Doctor.

"You *must* find this book as what other way is there for me to return to the asylum and to my family?" Matthew pleaded, eyes wide with an overwhelming anxiety that he had never known before.

"If we dig some more we may uncover it, let's keep going Matthew, *don't* give up hope, son!"

The sharp but rusty blade of the shovels clawed at the damp earth, every sinew and muscle fibre in their shoulders and arms screamed with the unrelenting ache of fatigue. They hit something hard and grinned at each other triumphantly.

"Oh please God, let it be The Book!" cried the young man, as glistening beads of sweat trickled down his forehead; blinding him momentarily. The Doctor crouched down and grabbed sods of earth frantically, his eyes ablaze with anticipation and curiosity. He broke a fingernail from scratching at the soil - and the sharp edge of a thick heavy metal box!

"Ouch!" "That fucking hurt!" he muttered as a droplet of blood began oozing from the freshly-cut soil-covered calloused skin. Matthew assisted him in pulling the box from the earth and they both used the edge of one of the shovels to prise the lid wide open. It groaned and creaked with the effort, and succumbed; displaying its contents in the afternoon sunshine that glinted on the lid. The Book was in there! They both laughed hysterically and sat together on the dirty ground - not caring if their clothing became matted with; grass, soil or anything else for that matter. They had *found* The Book!

They hid it under a jacket as they approached the Surgery.

"Nobody in the town can *ever* see this book, Matthew, do you realize the vast importance of everything within these pages?"

"All I care about Doctor is getting back home again." he sobbed. "My wife will be frantic by now, I *must* let her know that I'm alright, so, if there is *any* way that you can help me to return to my time, then I will be forever in your debt."

"Matthew, I will do all that I can to help you. Relax and trust me." "I am a Doctor after all and you are not the first person that I have helped to return to the future, and to come back here too, as a matter of fact, but you can *never* tell anyone that I have disclosed this information to you." "*Never!*"

Matthew nodded in agreement and they both sat down as they studied The Book. It described at length of spirits that attach themselves to, and, who live inside mirrors. They had the ability to use these mirrors as a portal, to drag unsuspecting human victims through them, with them - to another time - past, present or future. These spirits could be summoned but, there was a price to pay for doing so - the person would be followed around wherever they travelled.

Dr Evans opened a large cupboard and Matthew peered inside, trembling. Inside the cupboard, bolted to the walls of it - was a huge crystal-clear mirror. Beside it sat a sheet of paper with detailed information written upon it. It was entitled: *The Spirit Summoner.*

It told of a method of summoning powerful spirits who, could either assist - or harm another. Diagrams were depicted of how to conjure up these spirits and, in doing so, the person would from henceforth be eternally responsible for their actions - and the consequences were dire, to say the least - if the person betrayed the spirit(s); intentionally. Matthew's eyes widened in terror as they scanned every word, slowly. His heart raced as he digested the importance of the information. He looked at Dr Evans, who told him to close his mouth - as his jaw was practically prodding his chest.

"I will do whatever it takes to return to my time, to see my wife and kids" he said.

"Then brace yourself young man, because what you are about to go through, will shock you to your very core. I've been there myself and it aint pretty!"...

They both recited the words of an ancient sacred ritual and prayed to the Goddess who ruled the earth. They joined hands and sat near the mirror. The foundations of the building shook and began to vibrate powerfully. As they closed their eyes, the mirror began to morph into a fluid, animated, vision. Time seemed to suddenly speed up as every nerve and tendon within their bodies stretched to the max. Tension filled the air and compression affected their limbs to the point that they couldn't breathe. They gasped and continued to close their eyes; primarily out of fear and, also to block out the room that span around like a carousel - quickly spinning out of control. Out of *their* control.

In what appeared to be seconds, they found themselves back into the future - sitting outside the asylum by the fountain, which was situated at the entrance to the huge white building. They sat there gathering their thoughts, and breathed a huge sigh of relief. They had made it back! As Dr Evans slid The Book inside his jacket, they both walked towards the front door, looking at each other with suppressed hysteria. They couldn't let anyone see their exuberance; as others simply wouldn't understand. They could just about fathom it themselves...

~CHAPTER NINE~
Channelling in the basement!

Matron enjoyed her coffee break while in the middle of sifting and sorting through patient documentation. She rubbed her weary eyes. Gazing out of the window, she opened it a little to let in fresh air to see off the stale that had inhabited her room for the past few hours. She felt restless and fatigued. Deciding to go for a short walk, she packed up her things into her black leather handbag and slung a blue cotton scarf around her neck, to keep out the chill. Slipping into her black leather boots, gloves and a dark blue wool coat, she locked the office door and trotted towards the stairwell.

She avoided the elevator at all costs - since recent developments had occurred and, she vowed to herself that she would *never* travel ever again in one! As she stepped down each step; her boot heels clicking on every centimetre of stone, she felt good for the first time in a while and she sprayed herself with her favourite perfume. Inhaling the sublime fragrance she made her way to the ground floor.

As the chill in the air clawed at her cold skin, she turned up the thermostat on the wall by the Reception desk. The radiators produced a loud clanging sound and she cursed under her breath at the maintenance staffs' negligence. Writing down a reminder to contact them, she placed the piece of notepaper back into her bag. She looked good, and knew it; her black nylon stockings shimmered in the light as her long uniform swayed in an authoritative manner. She pulled on her leather gloves snugly and felt the leather caress her cold fingers.

She loved how the leather sounded when stretched. She was a Matron in a highly-responsible position but she was also a woman, with needs - and leather turned her on *so* very much. She had often glanced at Bob's leather gloves and, her body always reacted with an unbearable aching desire to feel his touch - even if just momentarily he touched her body - she would have damp panties, instantly. She smiled and thought of him, hoping that he was feeling back to his usual self after his scare in the elevator, and the resulting concussion afterwards, from his fall. He was often upon her mind;if only she realized how often she was upon his also...

The sun lit up the front entrance of the asylum like a warm gold-coloured blanket; totally smothering it in warmth and comfort. Claudia wrenched open the huge door and breathed in the fresh vibrant air. She coughed and spluttered. As a smoker, she had developed a hacking cough - that didn't help her neck problem one bit.

Lighting up one of her favourite menthols, she stood on the front step and, her tense shoulders relaxed instantly. As her soft wet lips sucked on the cigarette she wandered off within her imagination and remembered less stressful days. Days of worrying about nothing, days of having no responsibilities.

She smiled and recalled memories of long ago when she would sit on her parent's front porch and do her school homework; taking her time and enjoying the evening sunset as it disappeared on the horizon; much like her concentration level as her eyes fixated on the handsome boy that cycled past her house at exactly 6 o'clock each day. He looked much like Bob, but younger. She missed Bob when she didn't see or hear from him in a mere matter of hours. Unbeknown to her - he missed her twice as much!

She blew a haze of menthol smoke outwards and stubbed out the cigarette upon a stone lion that accompanied another that sat opposite it. She had always liked Leo men, they were adventurous, charming, likeable men - and oh so *very* sexy, she thought. Bob was the astrological sign of Leo, she was a Sagittarian - very compatible, like two red-hot flames aching to entwine their fires and exhibitionist tendencies...

Bob was in the basement; fiddling about with an electrical drill and repairing a mains socket. He felt powerful and manly whenever he fixed an appliance and, the kettle downstairs made not a jot of difference - if he could repair it then he was 'Boss.' He inserted a fuse into the compartment, twisted the appropriate wires around the inner metal components and placed half of the plastic plug back onto its adjacent partner; screwed it firmly back into place. It was fixed!

"Thank *God* for spare fuses!" "Now if Claudia has visitors I can at least have a coffee by myself as its bloody chilly down here!" he muttered to himself.

He hoisted up his trousers and brushed off the dust from his shirt. He prided himself on his appearance and tried to look smart at every opportunity - even if it were just he that noticed it. It filled him with a sense of pride, a sense of dignity - if he always looked his very best.

Matthew and Dr Evans walked past Claudia and she commented that they seemed unusually happy and that they had a spring in their step. They simply smiled and laughed as they trotted past her and into the asylum. She turned around and noticed a rather large bulge protruding out of the Doctor's jacket. He was oblivious to her noticing this and he closed the main entrance door behind him.

She walked over to the weathered stone fountain, a few feet away, and saw that the water had a film of stagnant slime starving the water from oxygen. It strangled all of the life out of the water and she wondered how on earth the birds would ever manage to wash their feathers in that; as she placed her hand inside the green gooey mess to agitate it in order to bring some life and oxygen into it.

She wiped the green sticky mess off her fingers with a white cotton handkerchief and threw it in a nearby bin. It slid down the inside of the bin in an almost lazy, sloppy manner. Her empty cigarette packet followed it. She noticed that in one of the upper-floor windows a ghostly-white face looked back down at her, then it disappeared... She assumed that she was working far too much and that her eyes were now deceiving her. She coughed, cleared her lungs and walked back inside the building. Brenda was throwing furniture around again and Jane was plotting her demise in her warped mind.

Mable, the canteen head cook was filling in the Menu form and fidgeting with her underwear, which chafed against her inner thighs. Tricia was wandering off down the corridor talking to herself and doodling on a sheet of paper as Matthew and Dr Evans discussed how to repair worn components in elevators. It was just an ordinary day - as far as Matron was concerned.

The minibus pulled up outside the asylum and the patients arrived safe and well - each clutching a bouquet of beautiful flowers which they were not allowed to keep in their rooms as it wouldn't surprise Claudia if one of them got hungry and decided to eat them.

Well, they would probably taste nicer than Mable's dismal cooking, she thought. They were to be displayed in the nurse's rooms and in Matron's office.

Brenda, Jane and Tricia had returned early due to ill-health, and relished the peace and quiet as the other patients were noisy on the best of days; let alone on the worst of them. Claudia chatted with the nurses about the following morning's activities and shared a cup of coffee with them in the main office. They noticed that her filing cabinet had been padlocked.

They whispered among themselves as to what could possibly be in there; maybe Matron's new vibrator lay hidden in there, they thought. She hadn't had sex in decades, so it would be a possibility. They winked at each other behind her back and she was oblivious to their low level of administering the due respect towards her. She scratched her hip and winced as the tight elastic in her panties irritated her - far more than her essential daily responsibilities *ever* could, she thought.

Bob sauntered past and smirked, as nobody else had noticed her fidgeting - but *he* had. He vowed to get her an erotic assortment of lingerie for her birthday in a few days time and hoped that she wouldn't be offended; but would be ecstatic at his thoughtful gesture. The lust and romance between simmered all day long, so her birthday would be the candleflame of a fulfilled hot desire if she appreciated his gift in the way that he anticipated that she would. A kiss on the cheek would devastate him. He preferred and hoped for *so* much more... He could wait, he thought, as she was worth the wait. What would another day matter - when she had been the object of his love, lust and desire for decades.

Mable poured herself a cup of coffee in the canteen and sat on a wooden stool, collecting her thoughts. She wiped off a smear of baked bean juice from off her pinny and placed her palms on the tops of her knees; relaxing her mind and body completely. She closed her eyes and slowed her breathing. She knew about relaxation techniques from her study of Holistics books and enjoyed practising the suggestions whenever she had a chance.

As she relaxed and her body sank into the seat, she felt a featherlike touch on the side of her left cheek. It didn't startle her enough to get her to open her eyes, she had thought that it was a slight breeze as one of the canteen windows was open. It occurred again, this time more forcibly. She opened her eyes to see that the cutlery that she had been soaking in the sink to now be arranged side by side upon the counter top.

She smiled as it had occurred on many occasions over the years so she wasn't fazed in the slightest. She knew that spirits existed in other dimensions and on many astral planes as she had seen her grandmother on many an occasion. The other canteen staff walked in, their chatter strained her ears and destroyed the peace and quiet that she had been enjoying for the past hour.

"Hello ladies, we have a new menu to prepare today, Matron's orders!"

"What is the new inclusion on it, Mable?" asked Sophia. She removed her coat and hung it upon the hook on the wall along with the others.

"Would you believe it, she wants lasagne back on the bloody menu!"

They all rolled their eyes as they loathed the meaty concoction but, they knew that if they were to remain in her good books - they would have no option other than to get on with it. They washed their hands and set about preparing the said disliked meal. Holding a spoon in each of their mouths they peeled and chopped a lot of onions and they had discovered that this was the only way to prevent the tears from streaming down their faces. They each smirked and chuckled in unison as the spoons hung from their clenched teeth.

Dr Evans and Matthew approached Bob near the elevator and asked him if he was prepared to engage in some channelling with him. He had read of such a thing and they explained to him at length exactly what it entailed; drawing spirits to you and through you in order to communicate messages to each other or for another person.

In The Book it described in graphic detail the consequences of doing this and that proper grounding techniques were to be adhered to at *all* times - to protect themselves. It involved visualising tree roots wrapping themselves around a boulder deep in the earth's core and then travelling upward; wrapping themselves around the person's ankles. Following this, the person was to visualise a cascading enveloping white light coming down upon the person and filling them up inside too. Then channelling could commence - with the person being safe from any negative spirits harming them.

They were each terrified of engaging in this activity but knew enough to know that it was a safe procedure, *if* followed properly. As they stood in the elevator and closed the door, they prepared themselves for whatever would happen. Their heartbeat quickened and they trembled. Nothing happened. The huge mirror behind them on the elevator wall began to shimmer and a deep groaning came from within it. It startled them to the point that they grasped each others hands tight in order to strengthen and to reinforce the circle that they had created.

"Now gentlemen, don't feel embarrassed as I can assure you that I am heterosexual and am not remotely interested in either of you!" said Bob.

The two men looked at the floor and felt their faces becoming red and hot. They grinned and stifled a laugh.

"Bob, we can assure you that we are also not interested in men, so no worries there!" "Let's continue and focus".

"The spirit that we are aware of who is haunting this building and is causing strange things to happen, please show yourself. We mean you no harm and only wish to find out exactly what your intentions are regarding us - and this town".

Nothing happened. They waited. Then they waited some more. Just when they thought to call it a day and to end the channelling, they noticed that the elevator began to move; slowly at first, then it increased its speed. In passing each floor, the walls of the elevator changed in appearance; paint peeled off them and even the light above them altered from an electrical fitting to a gas glowing brass lamp. Their clothing changed into that of centuries long ago and all the while that this occurred, at no time did they let go of each others hand.

They were ashen-faced with terror and they could each hear the pounding of their heartbeat in their ears. Then, the elevator ceased to move. An old wooden door lay before them. Even the buttons on the wall had disappeared. They were in another time, another life. They gripped the huge brass handle of the door and slowly turned it. As the door creaked open eerily, bright sunlight shone upon their frightened faces.

"I think we can all let go of each others hands now gentlemen!" said Dr Evans.

They exhaled an enormous sigh of relief and walked forwards. The old village teemed with life before them; wooden carts dragged boxes of items across the dusty pathways and people chatted in the distance, going about their day. Bob told them about the old house up the lane that nobody ventured near and Dr Evans informed him that he had known all about that place for longer than he cared to remember. Matthew asked them who lived in that house and was told that all would be revealed in due course.

As the three men strolled around the village; waving to people and purchasing foodstuffs for their journey, Bob looked around for the beautiful lady that had caught his eye previously when he had ended up there the last time. There was no sign of her. He felt a little sad. As they approached the lane to the dark creepy house, they peered around to ensure that they hadn't been seen by anyone else. The house had a depressing look to it and the apprehension that filled the men almost overwhelmed them to their core.

They resigned themselves to the fact that there was no going back now; they had reached the point of no return. They just had to know who lived there and why their ominous presence followed them around. The building was still, as was the general atmosphere now. The door seemed to loom upon them and increase in size dramatically - such were the tricks their fatigued minds were playing up on them.

"Bob, you knock, you're the bravest among us!" pleaded the two men. But Bob's hands were shaking to the point that he couldn't button up his jacket let alone summon up the ability to knock on a door.

"I'm sorry guys, you'll have to do it, I'm too nervous." his eyes pleaded with unsaid requests of forgiveness from them for his unmanliness. Normally he was a courageous man, but in this instance his nerves failed him dismally.

Dr Evans and Matthew both agreed that they would knock on the door, together. As they did so, it creaked and ever so slowly it opened - millimetre by millimetre. The wait was excruciating for them all, so, to hide their 'unmanly' fear they all pushed the door ajar to silence the creepy creak. Bare floorboards lay before them, quietness and the stillness were deafening.

They warily crept inside and held their breath. Peering around the corner of a doorframe they noticed that a fire roared away in a granite-black fireplace. Several cats snoozed on a desk opposite - oblivious to their presence; although the ears on each of them twitched slightly and moved in different directions. Maybe they were used to people checking out the premises, or maybe they knew what to expect when an intruder dared to walk in...

An elderly lady hummed a tune and chatted away to herself in the corner. She *knew* they were there of course, but pretended not to notice their presence. She wanted to see what they would do and what they'd say to her. They stood there for what seemed to be centuries in time - but were mere seconds; deciding what questions to ask her. She spared them the agonising wait and turned around, piercing their silence with a stern stare.

"Hello gentlemen, what can I do for you on this fine day?" she asked. She continued to sew a garment; her nimble fingers worked away at a frantic pace with an almost hypnotic rhythm.

"Erm...hello...we need to ask you some questions if you don't mind?" they said, nervously.

"What kind of questions would those be then?" she asked inquisitively - already knowing them. She was psychic after all and possessed many powers that only Dr Evans was aware of but, so as not to instil the fear of God into the other two men, he kept silent.

She knew him and didn't let on to the others that she did so. A half-smile crept along her aged features slowly, and she beckoned them all to make themselves comfortable and to sit on the sofa. Ordering the feline companions to make a scarce exit from off it, she dusted the cushioned seats down to make them appear more presentable to the men.

They didn't really want to take up too much of her time but felt driven to find out more from her, so they warily sat down and relaxed as she offered them a pot of coffee. They declined; anxious that she would poison them and that they would never been seen ever again. God knows if she had corpses down in the basement or buried underground - they assumed. As Bob and Matthew took in the room, looking around to find evidence of missing persons and so forth, Dr Evans whispered to her that he had found The Book and that he suspected that she had taken it when he was distracted. She denied this and shook her head defiantly.

"Look here, I *know* you took it, admit it!" he sneered menacingly, his eyes widening.

She avoided the subject and chatted with the men about the village and what a pleasant day it was that day.

Dr Evans fidgeted in his seat out of frustration, and sighed deeply. He resigned himself to the fact that she wouldn't admit her theft, so he let the matter go. Besides, the two other men wouldn't believe him so what was the *point* in mentioning it really, he thought. She glanced at him and momentarily grinned. This infuriated him so he decided to humiliate her in front of the others.

"So, tell us, what is your name and *why* are you a recluse in this bubbly vibrant village?"

She looked at the floor, gathering her thoughts.

"Many years ago, my brother disowned me. He spread gossip about me to the villagers, they turned on me; such was the high regard that they had for him - being a Reverend of the church and all - so I put a curse upon them all, the lot of them, and have lived her alone ever since!" "Well wouldn't *you* do *exactly* the same thing?" she asked, staring at them all one by one, her eyes narrowing with simmering anger.

Bob stuttered and cleared his throat from his building anxiety.

"What did they say about you...if you don't mind me asking?"

She stood up and paced around the room, agitated. Her shoes clacked on the bare floorboards - much like a dancer in warp-speed. As she muttered obscenities to herself under her breath about the villagers and, what they had done, she once again looked up and, hands upon hips, she told them of the ostracism that she had unjustly endured at their hands, how they had believed the Reverend over her kind warnings that spectral beings with malevolent intent lurked in and around the church, her own brother's disgusting avoidance of her, how they had formed a lynch mob that evening and had driven her out of the main town square.

"It's despicable what they have done to me, so I placed a curse upon them!" She threw her head back and laughed hysterically. "*I* am the person responsible for bringing you back here - whenever I choose to - and there's *nothing* you can do about it!" she screamed at them.

"But *why* do you want us here, what is your purpose in doing this?" they all asked at once. She looked at them and her facial expression seemed one of momentary remorse.

"You have three people working at the asylum who I once knew, and one of you sitting in this room doesn't realize who he is, and the powers that he has but, in due course...he will. *That* is why I visit the asylum, you see, I've been trying to tell this person that they are *not* safe there as demons are out to get them all!"

The three men looked at each other, each wondering who among them she referred to. Their minds went blank. Dr Evans knew it couldn't be him as his time was here, in the here and now - not in the future. It must be Matthew or Bob - as they were of the future. The witch transfixed her stare into Bob's eyes and the hairs on the back of his neck stood bolt upright instantly. He felt as if his heart would burst out of his chest at any second.

"It *can't* be me, I just work at the asylum carrying out maintenance there," he said. He nervously played with the pocket on his jacket and fidgeted in his seat.

She smiled and turned her attentions to Matthew. He gulped and coughed. The lump of fear in this throat seemed to want to tear its obstruction right out of his neck. He placed his hand upon his mouth and excused himself as he cleared his throat by coughing repeatedly.

"What is your name my child?"

"It's Matthew, what is yours?"

She told him that her name was one that they would all find out when they ventured back into the future. She explained that all would become clear and would make complete sense after they had left her presence that day and, they were not to worry themselves about anything. Despite their incessant nagging, she refused to disclose any further information.

"Make sure that The Book *never* leaves your side" she said - as she glared at Dr Evans. "It is of the *utmost* importance than nobody that resides within the asylum of Mordithax ever lays their eyes upon the words that are contained in this book, or there will be dire consequences for you all - if it falls into the wrong hands I mean...do you understand?"

They bid her farewell and went on their way. The cats followed them outside and the old witch stood in the doorway; almost wetting herself from her cackling laughter as she observed the grown men scurrying away like terrified little lambs going to a slaughterhouse. "What fucking wimps!" she muttered.

"We will return to see you another time m'lady," Bob said, as he tipped his hat and thanked her for the information that she had reluctantly given them.

"Oh trust me, I will see you a *lot* sooner before you see *me* again!"...she whispered to herself.

The men found their way back to the elevator and Dr Evans reversed the procedure that would transport them back to the future - to the asylum. He clutched The Book for dear life and vowed never to let it out of his sight, not even for a second, *this* time.

41

~CHAPTER TEN~
Someone has some explaining to do!

Claudia patrolled the corridors. She was in no mood for nonsense that day as it was *'that'* time of the month. She always felt grumpy for days and didn't hesitate for one moment to hide her obvious discomfort. The patients kept quieter than usual when Matron was in one of her pms 'moods'. Even Mable the head cook steered clear of her and had been known on more than one occasion to hide under the stainless-steel counters - for a quiet life.

Claudia shuffled along the corridors; adjusting her pantyhose and underwear for maximum comfort as she had a very long workshift ahead of her and would rather be anywhere else than there - even if she did love her job and prided herself on maintaining an efficient and impeccable asylum. She had a pristine reputation to live up to and not even menstruating would prevent her from doing her work - as far as she was concerned! If others were affected by her grumpiness then so be it. She thought they were a load of miserable bastards at the best of times and, today was no different.

Her bra straps dug into her shoulders, adding to her downbeat demeanour. She inspected each of the patients rooms and filled in her chart which recorded; their general attitude, *if* they had taken their medication and how well they were behaving that week. She monitored everything - right down to their physical appearance. She would not tolerate shoddiness in her asylum; not even unbrushed hair would be left unscolded.

Tricia sat drawing doodles and remained silent as usual. Jane sat muttering to herself and, in her imaginary world, she plotted the 'death' of anyone that had spoken to her that week. Brenda attempted to lift some chairs from off the concrete floor but, found to her disappointment, that they were bolted rigidly to the ground. The other patients enjoyed a nap and so Claudia simply walked past onto the next room. The snoring grew deafening, adding to her irritation. She decided that she would go and visit Bob in the basement area. He was always there to offer her words of comfort and was superb at it, she thought.

Bob's work colleagues were playing cards in the storeroom. The door was locked and they sat cheering each other on, whenever they won; as well as cursing and mocking the victor - in jest of course, they all got along very well and the bond between them had been set decades ago. They left Bob out of their card games; they detested his efficiency in the workplace and felt that he wasn't 'one of the boys'. He was ignored. Not that it mattered to Bob of course, he was grateful that he wasn't part of their group as they bored him to tears most days. Sometimes he'd stand behind them whenever they clocked-in at the start of each morning and he simply kept quiet and out of their way, if at all possible. Claudia approached Bob and her tension faded as soon as she saw him.

"I'm feeling like shit today Bob, how was *your* weekend?"

"It was *very* unusual to be honest Claudia, I'd actually like to confide in you about it if you have a moment?"

He gestured for her to sit down on one of the seats that were stacked up by the wall and she rubbed her aching feet. "What happened then Bob, you can tell me anything, you *know* that by now." He sat beside her and looked around to make sure that none of his gossipping work colleagues were near - they wouldn't understand or believe his story anyway, so he would be wasting his breath even bothering. He grasped his head in his hands and shook it back and forth.

"Claudia, I doubt you would believe a word of what I'm about to tell you, but hear me out please as I have to tell *someone* what I've experienced, as either I imagined it and am going crazy or...it *did* happen, in which case I need you to see it for yourself as Dr Evans and Matthew could be deceiving me somehow or drugging me. These could be fucking hallucinations for all I know!" "I don't trust many people, you *know* that."

He explained to her exactly what had happened in the elevator; when he and the two men had performed a channelling of spirit and, that they had been transported back four hundred years to another time...when the asylum hadn't even been built. Back to a time when a village existed, where a witch lived up a dusty old lane - a recluse and hermit - ostracised and ignored by the townsfolk, what she had told him, Dr Evans and Matthew about one of them having knowledge of how things worked, of secrets, of things that she had refused to disclose to them - but that it would be revealed in due course.

He described the witch to Claudia and that she had had a brother; a Reverend, who had preached in the church about his sister's beliefs in the supernatural and, all things of a ghostly nature of which were detested by he and the churchgoers to the same degree. How he had turned the congregation and the villagers against her and how he, her brother, had eventually disappeared. She had for a while but, was found to be living alone on the outskirts of the village. But *where* was he?...

Claudia tried to take in everything that he had told her and she stifled a laugh. She had no intention of mocking him as she loved him dearly so, she simply put her arms around him and reassured him that everything would be alright.

She felt his toned muscular body as her fingers pressed a little harder and he sank into her embrace. She felt his hot breath on her neck and her body ached for his intimate touch. She closed her eyes and sighed. As he wasn't courageous enough to make the first move she decided that she would instead. She turned her head slowly and noticed the bristle on his chin and upper lip - it only made her want him *more*. Her hands moved upward, toward his head, and she ran her fingers lovingly through his dark soft hair.

He looked at her and, for a moment, it felt as if time had stood still, as if all that mattered in his world at that precise second was drowning in her beautiful eyes - and he had no intention of desiring to be saved...*ever*. She had a power and a control over him that no other soul that he had ever met, had. Her soft lips met his and they both felt their knees weaken a little. He forgot time and space and all that lay inbetween as her mouth caressed his. She felt warm, light, and he felt like a god - because she wanted him. His Goddess wanted him, there and then.

Out of all of his work colleagues - she wanted *him* and him alone... As his hands wandered down towards her hips, he felt the blood engorge within his cock...and he didn't care if she felt its obvious sudden appearance. He wanted her. With all of his heart, soul, body, he wanted her, *so* very much that it became unbearable.

She felt his tongue eagerly search for hers and she responded instantly. Her nipples grew erect and her pussy dripped consistent dampness. That moment felt like no other that they had ever experienced in their lives. The passion, the heat, the overwhelming desire, unbridled lust and precious love - that they had felt for *so* very long, was now declaring itself in that moment. It was almost too much for either of them to bear, but they couldn't prise themselves apart from each other, not just for that moment; but not ever. The all-encompassing love that they allowed themselves to show each other was everything to them - and nothing else mattered, now.

Bob's walkie-talkie crackled in his jacket pocked; bringing him back to his senses, abruptly. He cursed it in his mind silently as his lips broke away from hers. He smiled at her; the love within his heart as he looked into her eyes was almost too much to contain - he wanted to shout it from the rooftops, how so very happy he felt at that moment. She gazed into his warm brown eyes and reciprocated. No words were required now.

They knew they had both made a breakthrough, they both knew that each adored the other and now it was out there in the open so to speak, it was admitted, it was *real* - and not a figment of their imagination, any longer. They were certain now.

"I'm going up to the main office, Bob, I'll talk to you later."

"Ok, I'll see you after work for our regular drink and chat. By the way, I..." his voice trailed off and his words of love were detained in a prison of fear - by his nervousness. She nodded.

"Me too, Bob" she said. She wouldn't ever force him to say those three special words. All in good time when he's ready, she thought.

As she walked up the stairwell, and her dress disappeared out of sight, he cried. The overwhelming relief became too much, tears of gratitude poured down his face. "She loves me!" "She loves meeee!" he repeated, over and over, reinforcing it, concreting and cementing the fact into place deep within his mind and heart. He dried his tears and whistled a tune as he strolled down the corridor, twirling a screwdriver in his hand as an electrical socket needed repairing.

He could still feel his lips tingling from her electric touch, and he grinned from ear to ear. He crouched down and began to dismantle the electrical socket; taking great care to ensure that the electrics were switched off in that area. He had carried out this job so many times than he cared to remember. What he didn't expect was the impending shock of his life - literally... He saw sparks shoot toward his face. In a split-second, he ducked, but, it hit the side of his neck; rendering him unconscious, convulsing.

He didn't have time to scream. Hours later he woke; confused and disorientated. He sat up and rubbed his head and neck; slowly coming around and gathering his bearings. He stared at the wall and wondered how could electricity be active from a switched-off power socket. A disgusting horrible smell of burnt plastic and rubber - similar to a fishy odour - filled his nostrils; reducing him to a choking wreck.

He retched and covered his nose and mouth with his trembling hand. He slowly stood up; swaying on his feet, and walked to the bathroom; holding the wall to steady himself as he did so. In the mirror, he noticed a burn mark etched into the flesh upon his neck - with the words:

'Come back!' 'Talk to me again!'

What could this mean? he wondered. The soreness was not half as bad as the pounding headache that repeatedly smacked his temples. He thought it wise to go and see Claudia; she'd know what to do to treat this injury and besides, he thought it best to get out of this basement before anything else happened to him! Not fearful by nature usually, this time he felt scared. *Very* scared. Someone, or something, had latched onto him and, although it seemed ludicrous to admit it to himself, he sensed that he was being targeted.

As he approached Claudia's office, he looked through the window of each of the patients' doors. Some were sleeping, some were reading, one wasn't on her bed. He peered in closer and banged his forehead on the door as Jean's face sneered before him as she loomed in from the side.

"Christ, what the fuck!" he squealed, and hurried towards the office, rubbing his head. Another bruise, great! He tried the handle on the door - it refused to open. The office must be empty, he thought.

As he began to walk past the room, he heard a familiar cough. Ah, so she *is* in there then! Through the window he could see that she was avidly reading through some patient files. She seemed to be so engrossed in this that she was oblivious to him gazing at her. He decided to leave her alone and went back to the basement. As he stood in the elevator he combed his hair and glanced into the mirror before him.

He thought that he didn't look too bad for a man in his forties and the fact that his woman loved him reinforced his belief that despite waiting decades to discover love, it *does* happen - eventually. She had put a spring into his step, a joy within his heart that he had never encountered before in his entire life; not even when receiving a bonus from overtime at work.

He smiled into the mirror and then a face that wasn't his - smiled back at him... As his eyes and mind adjusted to this spectral intrusion, before he had time to open the elevator doors and to make a sharp exit, a ghostly cold hand grabbed the collar of his shirt and pulled him back in. This time he didn't become unconscious and he found himself somewhere else in a moment. This time he stood and watched an invisible finger write something on the condensation that clinged to the mirror:

"I know who you *really* are...Reverend!"

As his mouth fell open and his eyes fixated upon the stern message, he felt intimidated and helpless.

"*What* do you want from me for Christ's sake?" he shouted, partly terrified and partly angry as things were starting to get on his nerves now to the point that he didn't know just how much more he could take of this nonsense.

He still wondered if he had become delusional and were experiencing hallucinations as the workload can take its toll on a person, but this was something else! He continued to stand still for fear of being dragged back inside again. He watched and waited. The mirror was wiped clean and this time another more threatening message ever so slowly crept its way across the glass - creating a screeching sound:

"If you go into the canteen, you will discover your destiny and *who* you really are!"

Bob stared into space and felt his heart quicken. He didn't have much time to decide how to respond to this situation so he made the decision to go outside for a few minutes to gather his thoughts and to have a much-needed cigarette.

As he opened the elevator doors and winced, his expectation of a repeat occurrence was denied; nothing happened, no creepy hand pulled him back this time, he was free to go. He raced up the stairwell onto the ground floor and ran outside; gulping in lungfuls of fresh air. He sat on the steps and searched for his cigarette lighter that was normally in the top pocket of his crisp white shirt. It had been moved. He rifled through all of his pockets and eventually found it in the back pocket of his trousers. *That's odd,* he thought. Lighting up his cigarette, he felt the tension ease out of his shoulders and back.

He closed his eyes and blew smoke rings from his mouth; oh how he thoroughly enjoyed an occasional cigarette, sometimes even a cigar, while enjoying a good film on the television. He loved to watch Claudia smoke. She would wrap her crimson-red lipstick-covered plump soft lips upon the cigarette end and the way she held it in her fingers always turned him on to a degree that no porn film *ever* could. She'd purse her lips and inhale the smoke *so* seductively, that a man could go mad just observing this 'sexually-charged' act. To him it appeared sexual of course. *Everything* that she did appeared sexual to him...such was the powerful effect that her presence had had upon him - for years.

Mable from the canteen saw him from the window and decided to join him for a smoke. The canteen was empty for now and a five minute break wouldn't hurt, she thought. She walked towards him and lit up one of her cigarettes. There was a chill in the air so she wrapped her scarf around her shoulders and neck and buttoned up her long green coat.

"Hi Bob, how are you?"

"Oh hello Mable, I'm not too bad thank you, how are things going in the canteen. Is everything good for you lately?"

"It's not *too* bad thanks. Some of the patients have been getting on my nerves as usual with their food-flinging habits in full swing though. *Why* don't the nurses control them more!"

Bob chuckled. "That's why I go there when *they* are *not* there, Mable."

She rolled her eyes and they chatted about life, work, stress. He suddenly turned to her; with concern in his eyes, and asked her if she had ever encountered anything unusual in the asylum. She replied that she hadn't and quickly stubbed out her cigarette before it was even finished. She seemed nervous, he thought.

"Oh well, let's get back to work. There's no rest for the wicked as the old saying goes, eh Bob!"

He wondered why she had been in such a hurry to leave, especially when he had asked that particular question. She didn't really provide him with sufficient time to ask again, so he let it be - for now. But she definitely knew something.

As he let the fresh air clear his lungs, he felt that someone were looking at him. It was an overwhelming sensation that he were being watched. He turned around quickly to see that Mable was lurking near a window. She moved away to the side and hid behind a curtain. How strangely she is behaving today, he thought. His curiosity became unbearable now and he had to know *exactly* what she knew about the building and, anything else for that matter.

He shivered, not because of the cold weather either. It was a cold day, colder than normal. He made his way to the canteen area and vowed to extract as much information out of her as he possibly could.

She'd give him an answer to at least *one* of his questions, he thought. He was not taking no for an answer.

He realized that the door to the canteen was locked and he knocked on the glass to attract her attention. She didn't come to the door. He knocked again, this time much louder. There was no sign of her. He pretended to walk away and hid behind one of the thick heavily-lined curtains. He waited. A few minutes later he craned his neck to peer through the glass in a window within the door. Mable was sharpening some chef's knives and she had a smile on her face that chilled him to the bone.

Why is she smiling like that? he wondered. She suddenly looked up and stood there; knife in hand, staring at him with an expression upon her face that was one of a very unhappy and angry individual. He wasn't hanging around so, he briskly walked away and ran up the stairwell to the main office. The elevator was faster, but sometimes the exercise did him more benefit.

"Hi Bob, why are you in such a hurry?" asked Claudia as she walked up the corridor to check on the wellbeing of the patients.

"Something is going on Claudia and I urgently need to talk to you about it."

"Whatever it is it will have to wait as I have to fill in some paperwork and then to make sure the nurse's are organised regarding tomorrow's party for Mable as it's her birthday." "We can chat about whatever is bothering you later, after work." "For my birthday we can have a quiet one, just the two of us."

She touched his hand, smiled, and he nodded in approval.

Mable *knew* about the surprise party of course, as she had overheard two of the nurses discussing it that morning, when they thought that she wasn't in the building. She would keep quiet about it and would simply smile when alone. How sweet of them, she thought. Now maybe she would forgive them for not having the ability to control the patients whenever they played up in the canteen. She detested how they chatted among themselves at dinner - completely oblivious to the behaviour of the patients right under their noses!

She could do a much more competent job and run the asylum all by herself, she often believed. But being a nurse was not her destiny, being a head chef was. She adored her canteen and all the responsibilities that it demanded. She thrived on stress and hard work and always endeavoured to give it her absolute best - and always did. She thought nothing of sacking anyone that failed to live up to her impossibly-high standards of excellence in the workplace.

She could have been a professional psychic as her grandmother had the ability also, but, she instead had made the decision to become a professional chef - like her mother. Mother is always right, she believed. The psychic visions just wouldn't leave her though and despite her blocking them out constantly - they always returned...

She'd been aware of situations in the asylum that shouldn't be happening, for a quite a while, but preferred to keep it to herself, rather than to disclose what she had seen and heard. She wouldn't know where to start or if they would indeed believe her and, she wasn't prepared to be laughed at and mocked and to lose her credibility as a chef or as a woman for that matter. So she said nothing. But would watch, listen, remember, learn.

She often pondered on just how many others in the asylum knew what was going on in it, but felt it wasn't her place to go chatting among the patients or the nurses. She may lose her job and that would devastate her.

~CHAPTER ELEVEN~
A birthday party - with a painful surprise...

Balloons in every available colour adorned the asylum - apart from in the patients rooms as they would choke on them - for Mable's birthday party. She arrived a few minutes later than usual in the canteen, on purpose, to keep everyone waiting impatiently. She was always prompt for her workshift and was never late. Tardiness she loathed. But, on her birthday, she felt inclined to bend the rules a little as it was her day and on her day she could do whatever the hell she wanted to, she felt!

She also dressed herself in a long black smart diamonte dress and jewel-encrusted high heels for a change and thought it would be perfectly acceptable if she didn't wear her usual pristine-white chef's uniform and boring flat shoes. She had even applied make-up and had had her hair permed for her day. A spray of floral perfume was also one of her indulgences for the occasion; and she felt and looked - beautiful. She even managed to smile!

One of the nurses - Penelope, dared to comment that she looked radiant and asked who had replaced her, but Mable bit her lip and smiled respectfully. Besides, she would remember the nurse's sarcasm and would repay in kind when she was back to her usual moody self.

"Mable, a very happy birthday to you my dear!" they all cheered as they raised a glass of wine to her. They all clinked glasses and tucked into a feast that had been prepared by caters. Every delicious morsel that could be imagined adorned the huge tables: seafood cocktails, salad, crusty warm buttered bread, followed by a sumptuous succulent steak main course - with all the trimmings - and a delicious chocolate sponge and custard for dessert. Cheese and crackers were also provided, but everyone was simply too stuffed full to accept those so they politely declined.

Bob had unbuttoned the top button of his tight trousers to relieve the bloatedness and had left his white shirt untucked to hide the potential embarrassment of accidentally 'flashing' himself to everyone. Claudia had cream and chocolate smeared over her top lip, oblivious to this of course, but the patients giggled about it at the table opposite her. Bob *so* wanted to lick it off, but resisted. He gazed at her as he sipped a small whiskey and cola; the cubes of ice frosted the glass nicely and the sweet liquid slipped down his dry throat a treat.

He didn't get drunk or drink a profuse amount of alcohol often, but when he did, he thoroughly enjoyed it; especially his nightly tipple with her when they would get merry, knowing that the nurses were quite sober and available immediately if any of the patients were in need of assistance with anything. Some extra nurses were called to the asylum as way on an invite from the others, who were friends.

One of the patient's, Jean, threw a rather large piece of cake across the room, where it landed on the nurse's table with a soggy splat. Chocolate and cream flew in all different directions - some of it landing on Doris; the oldest of the visiting nurses. She glared at Jean and mouthed that she would discipline her later that evening. Jean just smirked and threw her head back, laughing hysterically. Doris wiped the dark mess from off her face and as she couldn't do much about the stains on her white uniform that were slowly spreading outwards, she would put on a clean one after the party had finished.

Tricia felt intimidated by Jean and remained silent. Brenda's chair had been bolted to the floor to prevent her from hurling it at anyone that got in the firing line if they walked past, and she was restrained with heavy-duty hospital-standard cuffs and a thick canvas straightjacket. The others spoon-fed her; much to her annoyance. Well, if she did play up she could expect to be controlled, they thought.

Claudia applied some more lipstick and tutted as she noticed the chocolate upon her top lip. She licked it off as Bob watched. Their eyes met across the culinary chasm of the tables. She grinned and looked down into her hand-mirror; purposely and slowly sliding the scarlet lipstick over the soft plump lips; aware that he relished every moment of her doing this - tempting him, teasing him, desiring him...

His body ached for her touch but it was not the time or the place for such lustful activities, he thought, so looked away before he would have to leave the room due to an embarrassing erection that would hold up the tablecloth - if he were requested to stand up for some reason - but being unable to. There was always the menu sheet to hold, he thought. The sexual tension filled the atmosphere and he would have to leave, soon. Mable saw everything. She had an expression of jealousy on her face. Not because of their obvious blossoming relationship, but because if they knew of how complicated things could become if they got any closer, she would have to intervene rapidly.

Bob winked at Claudia and gestured for her to accompany him upstairs. She nodded and closed her handbag with a quick snap of its clasp. Mable scowled and turned her attentions to chatting with the nurses regarding the following mornings breakfast choices. Brenda pulled at the strong restraints that bound her limbs and attempted to shout; which was soon silenced by a mouthful of custard. Spluttering, she spat some of it at Tricia, who was more distressed that it had landed upon her drawings, than upon her clothing.

"Will you *behave*, for God's sake!" she shouted; out of character for her to do so, but she valued her artwork and soon found her voice if it was unappreciated by anyone else. Penelope noticed that Mable scowled at her so she sat next to her and apologised for her lack of sensitivity regarding her unkind comment that she had made earlier.

"Oh I've forgotten all about it Penelope, no harm done. It's fine," she said. But, she seethed inside. Grinding her teeth with anger, she forced her jaw to relax as one of her fillings had managed to work its way loose lately and she didn't relish crunching it up with a morsel of cheese, later.

Upstairs, Bob walked behind Claudia and admired the sway of her curvaceous hips as she tottered in her heels to the office. She locked the door behind them and they embraced, sinking into the sublime feeling of familiar touch. *Chocolate is heaven on a plate,* she thought, but being in his arms surpassed that and then some. *If that feeling could be bottled they would be multimillionaires,* he thought.

They closed their eyes and simply stood there, her arms around his neck, his around her waist, their cheeks touching, the sensation of bliss was undeniable between them. His left hand wandered down toward her thigh and she gasped. He promptly silenced it with his eager mouth. Her lips were *so* inviting; as was the intoxicating fragrance of her perfume. He felt himself becoming one with her, sinking into all that she was; the woman of his dreams, his love - his very purpose for being alive.

She felt a tear trickle down her cheek, and she smiled. She had never experienced love like this before; all those before him were insignificant now in comparison to him. Her Bob. His fingers trembled as he felt her warm skin beneath her dress, her suspender straps excited him to the point that his knees almost buckled as he trailed one finger along the black fabric. He didn't wander too far upwards out of his deep respect for her but she led his hand to an even warmer softer place where his hand lingered for a while before he let it gently rest on her inner thigh.

"C'mon now Bob, I think we know each other *very* well by now, don't you?"

She moved his hand higher, he felt the lacy edge of her panties and his cock ached to pleasure her, to surrender to her urges, to succumb to her lust. She wanted him, but he felt unable to make the first move. She would have to take the lead - preferably before he got to bursting point. That sticky mess would be far more interesting than a thrown splat of custard from Brenda, he thought.

51

The sexual tension in the air crackled. His breathing became laboured and he panted. She arched her back and slipped his hand down into her panties - ever so slowly - until he could take no more. He gripped her lower back with one hand and pulled her into him passionately. She ran her fingers through his hair as their bodies entwined in their mutual lust. They yearned to make love, right there and then.

She undid his tie and shirt, revealing a toned lithe body. His racing heart was evident by the pulse in his neck; coinciding with the waves of pleasure spreading across her wet pussy. She lifted up her arms as he gently removed her beautiful dress. He folded it but she grabbed it from him and threw it onto the filing cabinet. No time to waste, she thought. She wanted him there and then!

He gazed at her lacy full bra and the curves of her voluptuous body mesmerised him. She lay on the tartan patterned carpet and pulled him towards her, grinning. He lay on top of her and groaned. She unzipped his trousers and felt his large cock probe the entrance to her pussy. She didn't bother to use a condom as neither of them slept around and were too old they thought, to have children. Besides, she had been sterilised decades ago due to choice, rather than necessity. She still suffered pms-type symptoms monthly however, mainly psychological.

She guided him into her as she parted her lips in complete and overwhelming surrender. At that very moment she could do absolutely *anything* - and he would agree to it - such was the power she held over him. As they made slow passionate love, time seemed to stand still and nothing mattered but the two of them celebrating their love. As their mutual orgasms ripped through their bodies, Claudia felt herself lose consciousness several times due to the overwhelming surge of emotion from it all.

Hours later, they caressed each other lovingly as they sipped brandy and savoured every precious second together. They felt as equals despite their very different positions in employment. They felt so at ease in each other's company and lighter than air, for the first time in their lives. Chatting about their families and reminiscing about lost opportunities they sat side by side and thoroughly enjoyed each other's company.

He disclosed to her that his wife had previously been a patient at the asylum and that she hadn't even recognised him as her mental conditions had deteriorated over time, before her death finally dissolved their connection to each other. Claudia consoled him. As they held each other close and, oblivious to the chatter and partying downstairs, they decided that they would spend the night there in the office on a pull-out sofabed. Besides, it would be so much fun, she thought...to discover if he snored or talked in his sleep!

He thought the same - but didn't say a word. As they cuddled under the blanket on the sofabed, giggling like children while tickling each other mercilessly, they only moved to use the toilet and to make coffee. The heater was on full blast but the warmth from each other was more than sufficient to ensure that they would remain cosy and content.

As they grew tired and settled down for the night, they didn't notice a shadowy figure lurking outside the door, its presence unheard by both of them. They were in their own little world right now and had forgotten previous eerie events. The shadowy figure hadn't however, and was intending to stir things up a bit to say the least...

As the nurses led each patient to their room, the lights were switched off; apart from the main security one in the corridor. Penelope shivered and wrapped a wool shawl over her shoulders as she paced around making sure that all was ok and the women were settling down to sleep. She felt something touch her leg and she put her hand over her mouth to stifle a scream, not wanting to upset the patients who were already hyper after the party.

She ran down the corridor and upon seeing that the office light was out she decided to accompany the other nurses downstairs. She didn't get very far as unseen hands pushed her down the stairwell. She hit her head on a wall at the bottom of the steps. Her face made contact with a small window - breaking her nose and cheekbones in the process. Upon the hard edges of each step, leg bones cracked, then broke; resulting in her laying in a crumpled heap on the cold floor.

She suffered multiple injuries and wasn't discovered until an hour later when the other nurses went upstairs to check on her whereabouts and why she was late coming to see them, as arranged. Whimpering and semi-conscious, battered and bruised, she was barely alive - but alive she was.

As the Paramedics arrived to transport her to hospital, the only sense that they could get out of her were incoherent mumblings about feeling the sensation of hands pushing her. Finger-shaped bruises were discovered on her upper back with scorch marks along her lower back and legs; deep lacerations in her skin indicated that someone had also scraped a sharp object along her body. Forensics tested for skin and hair DNA evidence but none were found. They were mystified and baffled, but they kept her in for long-term observation and arranged to have psychologists analyse her when she felt up to it. They were determined to discover exactly what had happened to her and an investigation was opened.

Life went on as usual in the asylum, but all of the nurses were under strict orders to work in pairs; *never* to be alone - anywhere in the building. They visited Penelope whenever they could. Mable was the only person that didn't. Claudia felt guilty. If she and Bob hadn't been in the office, sleeping, they could have changed the course of events, possibly.

Filled with guilt, she vowed to be vigilant from there on and would only spend time with Bob when the safety of everyone else was assured.

In the hospital, Penelope woke from her coma and was promptly sedated as her screams were continuous. The poor woman - severely traumatised from her experience - insisted on never returning to the asylum in future. She'd simply get another job elsewhere.

~CHAPTER TWELVE~
Misleading answers

The following afternoon, Dr Evans shared lunch with Bob in the canteen. The other security guards sat at their usual table opposite, their gossip clearly heard by everyone in the room. No attempt to contain their thoughts and accusations to a whisper, they voiced their opinions without concern.

"Dan, but it *must* have been Mable who pushed Penelope down those steps. She never got on with her - so it's obvious!"

"Don't be so stupid, Mark, if that were the case the Forensics team would have some kind of DNA evidence as even the tiniest particle of skin can implicate an attacker nowadays."

The other men sipped their coffee and remained silent. They had had enough of listening to it all; hour after hour, and thought it best to now stay out of it and to change the subject if possible. But Dan and Mark persisted in debating the incident and neither would back down on asserting his opinion on the matter. Mable overheard every single word and carried on chopping some onions several feet away for lasagne mixture. She ground her teeth and felt the heat of anger build inside her as each accusation felt like the stab of a sharp knife in her ears.

She turned around and glared at the two men, wiping the blade of the knife in a tea towel. They were too engrossed in their discussion to notice however, but Bob noticed the expression on her face and frowned. Something is going on here, he thought. Dr Evans brought his concentration back by tapping his arm and asking him if he would like his remaining piece of lasagne.

"These onions are giving me the belches something rotten, Bob, they'll be repeating on me *all* bloody day now. *You* have them if you're still hungry!"

Bob politely declined and glanced at his watch. Time to get back to work, they thought. As Bob walked past the kitchen area, Mable smiled at him and thanked him for his company at the party and the compliments that he had given her regarding her new dress and heels. He responded by thanking her for appreciating his choice of birthday present for her; a new handbag. She told him that she would treasure it, always.

He did up the top button on his white shirt and straightened his tie. He rubbed the front of his shoes on the back of each trouser leg to shine them up some more and followed Dr Evans to the basement, where they intended on attempting another visit back in time to the village. Matthew would accompany them also as he found the entire experience so bizarre that he *had* to explore it further.

"Gentlemen, have you ever heard of, or have you ever carried out - automatic writing?" asked Dr Evans, grinning.

The two men looked puzzled and affirmed that they had not; but were intrigued and wanted to experiment in any way that they could - if it meant solving the mystery of what was going on in the asylum - and to find out exactly who had attacked Penelope. As the Doctor pulled out a sheet of white paper from his briefcase and sellotaped it to a small table, he showed them a planchette containing a pen that was held in the middle of it. The pen point rested upon the paper, motionless - for the moment.

He explained to them that they were to ground and protect themselves firstly, then to ask the spirit world for answers to their questions; the pen would move and symbols or words would be written by the spirit(s); not by them. They also placed a fingertip gently on the edge of a planchette in the middle of a spirit board and proceeded to ask relevant questions; thanking the spirits in advance for any interaction and answers that they wished to provide.

"Hi, my name is Doctor Evans, can you please write a message for us. Tell us who is responsible for attacking that nurse, thank you."

The pen remained still. Their fingers trembled slightly with the mounting anticipation.

"Hello, my name is Matthew, could you please write a name".

Still nothing.

"This is Bob, hi, can you draw a symbol or any words please, to show us what is going on in this building - and why?"

The pen began to move... They gasped. It drew a symbol at first; of a woman's face. It had gruesome twisted features and what appeared to be a word alongside it:

M a b l e

"What about Mable?" "What does she have to do in connection to what has been going on?" asked Bob.

The planchette on the spirit board spelled out a name, repeating its reply:

M-A-B-L-E

The three men looked at each other and mouthed a silent conversation. They asked each other what the message meant; then shrugged their shoulders, baffled.

"Bob, it only seems to respond to your questions, so from here on *you* should ask for messages."

Bob nodded in agreement and continued inquiring. The pen wrote a sentence this time:

Ask Mable what is what. She knows fucking...EVERYTHING!

The three men waited for more, but after ten minutes had elapsed they assumed that the spirit(s) had nothing else to say. They photocopied the sheet of paper and kept both copies in the Doctor's briefcase, so that if one became damaged, they would have a duplicate.

"Right, I think that's it for today, gentlemen." They closed the circle and made their way to the canteen.

Mable was drying some dishes with a tea towel and hummed a jolly tune to herself. She was alone. The other staff had left for their coffee break and would return in fifteen minutes. The three men locked the canteen door and approached her.

"Hello gentlemen, did you enjoy your lunch today?"

"Mable, we need to ask you something, it's *very* important."

"I have a lot to prepare for supper this evening, so it'll have to be quick!"

She sat down at one of the tables nearby and they showed her what the automatic writing experiment had produced on the sheet of paper and, they showed her a series of photographs depicting her name spelled out on the spirit board.

"What is this?" she asked, a baffled expression upon her face. But, she knew perfectly well what it all meant...and who was responsible for the messages...

"Mable, we *don't* expect you to believe us, but we have just conducted an automatic-writing experiment in the basement and this is what spirit have shown us in response to our questions as to what is going on in this building." "*Why* are they giving us *your* name?"

She told them that she knew nothing and that she was quite bemused as to why her name came up. She worked in the canteen and that is all that she did on a daily basis. She kept her nose out of other people's business and simply got on with her duties to the best of her ability.

"What do you make of this face that spirit drew for us?" they all asked in unison.

"Gentlemen, I haven't a clue who that is in the drawing, but whomever it is they are certainly ugly and I wouldn't want to meet them face-to-face on a dark night, that's for sure!"

"Where were you, Mable, when Penelope was pushed down the stairs?" "I'm so sorry to ask this but the police and Forensics officers will be interviewing everyone in this building tomorrow morning, so, if you do know anything about the incident you *must* tell us, even if it's a tiny detail, if you heard or saw someone, you *have* to tell us, now."

"I was here at the party, and I have witnesses to this!" "We were *all* here, apart from Claudia and you, Bob!"

Bob blushed with embarrassment and cleared his throat.

"I, um, we were..."

Matthew and Dr Evans told her that Claudia and Bob were with them downstairs. But Mable knew otherwise. She had witnessed their flirtatious behaviour during the party and had lived her life long enough to know what the result of such behaviour would lead to. She had seen the CCTV footage for herself - as Claudia had forgotten to switch the camera off...

It was normally left on at all times for security reasons and Mable had had an extra key cut - for access to the main office whenever she liked. She would switch the camera off of course, whenever she sneaked into the office, then would simply turn it back on when back downstairs in the control room - to which she also had a spare key. None of the staff were ever searched as they had worked there long enough to be completely trusted. She had heard and seen enough to know that both Claudia and Bob were not just sexually active but were in love too. She reassured the three men that they had nothing to worry about regarding trusting her and that whomever had pushed Penelope down the stairs, it most definitely wasn't her.

As they unlocked the door and bid Mable farewell, Matthew and the Doctor grinned at Bob, then winked. He thanked them for covering for him and they each wandered off to carry out their work duties for the rest of that day.

Mable sneaked into the control room quietly on tip-toe and locked the door behind her. She switched on the recording from the previous few days and noticed that Claudia had had an overly and unusual interest in files, lately. She wanted to know what was in them and on the footage she knew *exactly* where Matron had hidden them too! It was cold in the control room so she didn't stay long in there.

Shivering, she turned the spare key in the lock and hid it at the bottom of her handbag, underneath a hole that she had made in the lining. Humming to herself, she walked back into the canteen and waited for the other staff to return. They would be helping her to prepare supper before they all returned home.

Later that evening, the aroma of freshly-baked bread filled the building; it was heaven on a plate, they thought. The patients and staff sat down to warm-buttered crusty bread, beef stew and dumplings and there was lasagne left over for those that wanted that. The temperature dropped dramatically; everyone shivered.

"Bob, will you have a look at those radiators again, they've been playing up all bloody day!" shouted Mable.

He checked them but they seemed to be working just fine. Confused, he reassured them that the coldness wasn't due to them malfunctioning. They could all see their breath as they exhaled.

A hazy mist lurked in the corner of the room and grew larger and larger. It was unnoticed at first, but one by one everyone in the room began to see it emerging from the shadows... Some of the patients screamed, some simply stared in silent curiosity.

"Oh relax, it's just the sunlight coming through the windows!" said Mable.

"Mable, it's not, it's moving toward us and increasing in size - sunlight doesn't *do* that!" "Besides, it's a grey colour and, if it were a foggy day then it would be fog, but it's a sunny day!"

As Mable walked towards the window, she muttered under her breath that nobody ever seemed to listen to her, she didn't seem afraid or hesitant - which confused some in the room - but then again she had always exuded a very laid-back calm attitude most days so maybe that was why she seemed unusually brave, as they wouldn't dare approach the area themselves. She walked up to the mist and through it.

Closing the thick heavy curtains she proceeded to turn around and walk back toward everyone, glancing into a mirror on the wall to adjust her chef's hat, she stepped into the mist and promptly disappeared into thin air - quite literally! The incessant questioning had got to her...so she had astra-travelled - for some peace and quiet.

"Where has she gone?" they all gasped, rubbing their eyes in bewilderment at what they had just witnessed.

The grey mist began to fade, then was gone. They all ran towards the wall and peered out of the window. The garden and grounds were empty. Even the fountain had no sign of life around it as birds or the gardener would frequent that area all day on and off. Everywhere seemed still and a deafening silence filled the air. On the floor was Mable's handbag. One of the nurses picked it up, noticing a hard object jutting out near the underside of it. She opened the bag and reached down to the bottom, feeling a hole in the lining. She pulled out two keys and showed them to Claudia.

"Soooo, she's been untrustworthy all along then has she, the little bitch!" "These are keys to the main office and the control room!"

Claudia gestured to the security guards to follow her to the control room immediately and to give her the footage of the previous few days.

If she could see Mable in the footage then she would know that she had been in the room - instant dismissal - plus it would silence Mable if she even dared to consider blabbing to everyone that she had enjoyed a frenzied passionate romp with Bob during the party... If there was no visual evidence, she could prove that Mable was making it all up; if ever she *did* blab and open her mouth about it all. When they got to the control room, the tape had been removed.

"Quick! Look on the floor, maybe it's dropped out!"

"Claudia, it's *not* on the floor, there is nothing on the floor." they said.

"Right, I want *all* of you to search every room in this asylum for that tape!" "*Don't* come back to me until you find the damn thing!"

They all scurried off to search for the tape while Claudia made her way to the main office. "I wonder if the little bitch has taken it there!" she whispered to herself, panting as she climbed the steps. She felt out of condition - and knew it. What with excessive smoking and not exercising enough, she needed to tone-up and sharpish!

She unlocked the office door and searched everywhere for the missing tape, but alas, it was not to be found. Carpets were turned upside down, the filing cabinets had their drawers pulled right out, the wardrobe in the corner was moved; every inch of the office was scrutinised and examined. A few hours later, everyone returned to the canteen for supper. Silence reigned in the room. The general feeling was one of trepidation and resentment. The canteen staff had prepared everything immaculately. Their standards were not up to that of Mable's however, and this was apparent immediately. Everyone hurried their supper and went back to their separate areas.

The temperature had lifted somewhat, but a chill was still felt; especially up the corridors and the stairwell area. Claudia puffed on a cigarette outside by the fountain as she admired the starlit clear sky. A few shooting stars swept across and the moon glowed brightly. Bob kept her company and their arms entwined as they blew smoke rings together, giggling like schoolchildren.

The nurses tended to the patients needs and requirements; administering their medications to ensure they would have a good night's sleep - which was more than anyone else in the asylum could hope for - anxiety was at its highest there. As the lights were switched off it was 'business as usual' and everything carried on as normal as it could be. The overwhelming tension in the air permeated every nook and cranny in the building it seemed and, even the birds that congregated near the trees within the grounds were absent that night...

~CHAPTER THIRTEEN~
Meanwhile, down in the basement...

The electrical wires fizzed and crackled behind the steel panels of the elevator, the light flickered on and off at regular intervals as rats scurried around in the cavities of the building; chewing on anything that they could get their tiny sharp teeth into. Ghostly hands picked them up one by one and squashed the life out of the creatures, slowly...

Their bones twisted and the air in their lungs created wheezing sounds as it left their hungry little throats. Fur floated to the floor as it was ripped out.

The dark spirits enjoyed their torment and were biding their time for human flesh to descend upon the area. They didn't have to wait long as one of the nurses wandered across the corridor to the storeroom to collect clean linen for the patient's beds. She heard banging sounds coming from the elevator and assumed that it was down to the pipes or something. She shrugged her shoulders and walked back upstairs. An ice-cold breeze followed her, sweeping around her legs as she climbed each step.

"Brr, it's bloody *cold* today in this God-forsaken building!" she said; as she continued upward toward the main office to speak to Claudia before she changed the beds.

A sharp ghostly fingernail etched its way down her calf as she moved her foot to the next step. She thought that she had caught her leg on the jagged metal that jutted out from the steel safety rails, so, she rubbed her leg. A trickle of blood met her hand.

Running up the steps now, she shivered as she glanced at her watch that hung from her uniform. She was on time, on schedule, wasn't late for once. Matron would approve, she thought. The dark spirit crouched in the corner by the upper row of steps and waited... Others accompanied it. Time ticked by and they returned to the basement to plot their next move. They had all the time in the world. Besides, four hundred years were merely a blip in time to them - eternity was a long time to exact revenge for the asylum having replaced their beloved church - so they could wait...

The bitterness that they each had allowed to fester, had changed them dramatically. When Reverend Charlie Thomas/Bob had abandoned them and they had died in the fire, they eventually rebelled against everything that they had been taught regarding 'love thy neighbour' and to 'be at peace with others', they had felt that all the decades that they had loyally sat in the pews; listening with rapt attention to the sermons, obeying every sacred commandment, it had all been an utter waste of time.

Now they wanted revenge. Now they craved justice! Now, they would get it...

Mable shielded herself from their view and watched them. She'd protect everyone. Or could she?

~CHAPTER FOURTEEN~
What's lurking in the storeroom?

The storeroom harboured lots of things; freshly-laundered linen for the beds, laundry powder and fabric conditioner, electrical irons, ironing boards, reams of paper, boxes of pens and pencils, a spare toaster, two spare microwave ovens, uniforms - washed and unwashed - in separate baskets, labelled, spare slippers for Claudia; as there wasn't room in the main office, seven umbrellas, yards of dust and a multitude of cobwebs - complete with various-sized spiders who overlooked the lot - like miniature sentry guards - seeing off any intrusions from flies.

The rat droppings and rat poison were concealed in a corner - so as not to startle the nurses that visited the room as they went about their daily duties in the asylum. The storeroom was next to the elevator...and there was a hole in the wall...

At precisely 6am, Claudia's alarm clock woke her from a disturbed night's slumber. She lay there for a while, under the purple satin sheets, and stared at the ceiling, gathering her thoughts. Her dreams had been invaded by disfigured faces and a sensation of claustrophobia. She felt jittery, agitated, and had a feeling that it would be a pretty shitty day.

She crawled out of bed, made a pot of strong coffee and sat by the kitchen table puffing on a menthol cigarette. Bleary-eyed, she sat back in the chair and sighed. Rain poured outside and the clouds cast a dark and menacing shadow over her kitchen floor - showing up streaks of bacon fat that had spat out of the pan the night before. She enjoyed late-night suppers and her waistline was evidence of this.

The radio provided a somewhat upbeat mood but, the general atmosphere was one of her not really desiring to go into work that day, at all. Her only motivation was to see her lovely Bob. A text on her mobile phone instantly broke her sullen mood. It was Bob; his flirtatious compliments brought a much-needed smile to her downcast face. He ended the text with a love heart symbol. She replied with the same, after telling him that she needed to talk to him and that a hug would be very much appreciated.

She showered and dressed, then applied some make-up and brushed her hair. Maybe a squirt of perfume would cheer up the mood, she thought. But even her wavy dark hair was irritating her, as it resolutely refused to stay in place.

As she set off in the car to the asylum, she nibbled on a piece of buttered toast, the sticky honey dripped onto her hand. One lick and it was gone. Savouring the sugary-sweetness upon her whiskey-furred taste buds, she fantasised about Bob's superb physique and how amazing his sweet, yet passionate, kisses were. He had left his shirt in the office - which she had taken home, his aftershave within the fibres of the cotton provided a source of comfort and companionship for her as she drifted off to sleep at night, alone in her bed. As comfortable as it was, it was *no* match for his warm embrace.

Her daydreams were interrupted suddenly, as the sun began to emerge from behind the grey clouds, glinting off the rear-view mirror, causing her to squint. Sunglasses soon put an abrupt stop to that and she continued driving up the motorway to the asylum.

Favourite songs on the radio transformed her grumpy mood into that of a humming positive one and, she smiled. Everything would be fine, she thought. But little did she know that everything was *not* going to be fine and it would be far from fine for quite a long time to come! Pulling up outside the asylum, she noticed that the stone fountain was not only working properly, for once, it was spurting twice the amount of water up into the air and at the height of at least ten feet! It's going to be one of *'those'* days, she thought, scowling.

Mable stood by the entrance, finishing off her cigarette. Her hair was up in a bun that morning and she seemed unusually happy. Claudia of course, was sceptical and her curiosity would find out why.

"Morning, Mable, you're back with us then and you seem full of the joys of spring this morning!"

"Good morning Claudia, I just had a good night's sleep that's all. I have a tendency not to sleep well most nights, so I feel on top of the world today, for once."

"I wish that I could say the same for *me* as I've had a *crap* night's sleep and feel bloody *awful,* but you know me by now, I soldier on, come what may, Mable!" "Where did you vanish to?" "*How* did you get back?"

"I astral-travel, Matron, we all do it during sleep, I just have the ability to do it anytime that I choose to. I can show you how...if you want?" Claudia muttered to herself; "She's on about bloody astral-travel now!" "I dreamed the whole thing!" Mable heard her and vowed to show her exactly how it worked - when she had a spare moment, which wasn't often.

As she opened the door and walked inside, Claudia was unaware of the sarcastic expression that had spread across Mable's face. They tolerated each other, but were polite at all times, as maintaining an air of professionalism was a must - to the both of them. They were both perfectionists in the workplace and kept their private, personal thoughts - to themselves as to exactly how they really felt about each other.

Claudia detested her suspicious attitude over just about everything and, Mable equally detested her involvement with Bob. The sneaking around and her efficiency and positive attitude to life grated on her. She was envious. Claudia sensed this and had put it down to downright jealousy; personality traits that she strongly disapproved of.

Having parents that had exhibited the same qualities toward their neighbours wealth, had instilled a deep-seated hatred within her for the shallowness of it all - when all that she had ever wanted was to be brought up receiving what *really* mattered - hugs, love and a family-atmosphere - which were denied. They were *real* wealth.

Claudia had *earned* her position as Matron of an asylum. She had earned her degree at university, many years ago. She had a right to hold her head up high with pride and it wasn't about financial status, to her. She had nice things of a material nature, but what truly mattered to her was helping and comforting those who needed it, those who were vulnerable. Mable completely missed this of course and only saw the perks and prestige of Claudias job - right up the top of the ladder. Supremely successful. Whereas she simply worked in the kitchen; despite being excellent at her duties. It wasn't enough for her. She wanted *more.*

Because she *couldn't* achieve more, she projected her resentment of her own life - onto Claudia. She stubbed out the cigarette on the wall and removed her coat. It was a humid day and, being in a hot kitchen would just add to her existing misery. Thank God for electric fans, she thought.

She adjusted her stockings that were slowly creeping their way down her legs; from being much too big, and she walked towards the kitchen. The blast of cool soothing air greeted her as she opened the door. The other chefs stopped chatting the very second that they heard her footsteps approaching them.

Bob, Matthew and Dr Evans were in the basement; setting up locked-off cameras. They would allow them to capture any unusual paranormal activity that occurred there.

Later that day, they would position many other locked-off cameras and night-vision equipment - all over the asylum. Motion-sensors would also be placed around the building; to detect even the slightest of movement, along with EVP meters that would record any spirit voices.

Matthew came up with the idea for also having a trigger-object experiment which entailed him drawing around an object, locking the door to that room and then seeing if a spirit would move the object - thereby proving their existence.

As they all completed the tasks one by one, they stopped to have a coffee break by the elevator entrance. It had been functioning fine that day and there were no complaints of unusual activity - apart from the fountain outside in the grounds playing up and spurting water at twice the usual force; landing on the trees nearby, snapping a few thin branches.

The three men felt excited at what, if anything, would unfold that week - but they also felt individually terrified at the prospect of inadvertently agitating any spirits that would be attracted to the building due to the increase of electromagnetic energy that would increase therein - and neither of them felt inclined to reveal how nervous they were, in case they became even more nervous as a result!

They kept their thoughts to themselves and just carried on with carrying out what they had to do. Besides, it took their minds off it all - by keeping as busy as possible. All of the patients were watched more than usual, to ensure that they wouldn't wander off and knock any of the cameras from off the tripods. If any spirit orbs were to be seen - or any light anomalies - it would all be captured on video and, photographs would be taken every few seconds also.

Tricia sat in her room; avoiding Jean. Jean banged on the walls to annoy Brenda who, was already in the throes of throwing her chair repeatedly at the wall in response. Joanne paced up and down her room muttering obscenities to herself - but the insults were aimed at anyone that could hear her. Janet, Mildred and Nicola whispered through the walls among each other; a mixture of insults, paranoid ramblings and, they then began shouting at the top of their voices. Sheila shouted at her other personalities - and at all of the other patients, relentlessly.

They sensed that something wasn't right that day and, as much as the nurses attempted to calm them down, nothing seemed to work on *this* occasion. Sedation was the only solution, thought the nurses, after discussing all of the options that were available to them.

They approached Claudia outside the main office and discussed the matter with her. She agreed that this was the best thing to do. She didn't want any of the paranormal experiments to go wrong - as she would hold the nurses responsible for any cock-ups. As they were each well aware that none of them were in her good books usually - due to being found smoking inside the building - they were already treading on eggshells around her, afraid to voice their opinion about anything, but they couldn't sedate the patients without her express permission.

As Claudia handed each of them the required dosage for each individual patient, they noticed that her usual immaculately-applied lipstick was smeared across her face. They held back a smirk and, when her back was turned, they winked at each other and mouthed the words; 'Bob's been kissing her again!' She, however, was oblivious to their infantile behaviour and sorted through some paperwork that required their signature.

As the patients were calmed down, restrained and sedated, the nurses locked each door and went downstairs to grab a breath of fresh air outside by the stone fountain in the grounds. Claudia approved of this as she wanted to speak to Bob as soon as possible.

She missed him when she hadn't heard from him in a matter of hours and ached to feel his arms around her again; to soothe her frayed nerves and also because she couldn't wait to see his beaming smile and beautiful sparkling eyes again. He missed her too of course, but was so engrossed in setting up the paranormal experiments that she had slipped his mind - but only momentarily - she was never quite far from his thoughts.

The other two men drew diagrams of the various rooms within the asylum and marked each area in pen as to exactly what piece of equipment was in a room and, what its purpose was there. If they were to be successful in capturing any supernatural occurrences on film, they would have to do everything properly, efficiently and thoroughly. Mirrors were put up on every wall in the building and flour was sprinkled along every floor- to trap any ghostly 'footprints'.

If any spirit footprints appeared, the motion-detecting camera would immediately take several photographs afterward - trapping the culprit - resulting in concrete evidence for any paranormal officials and parapsychologists to analyse. Dr Evans knew his stuff; he had been a parapsychologist before becoming a psychologist in a different role but, had always felt that his earlier learnings would come in handy in the future. Now was that time.

With utter glee, he relished everything that he and the other two men were doing that day. Although prior sceptics, Matthew and Bob were slowly becoming convinced that there really *was* an afterlife. They all just had to prove it to everyone else - a daunting task, but, a task nevertheless, one that they felt was crucial if all paranormal activity within the asylum was to cease, once and for all. Bob longed to go back in time to see Becky again; the dark-haired beauty that reminded him of a younger Claudia, but Claudia was more important to him now and he resigned himself to the fact that he had enjoyed his brief encounter with the younger lady but, she was in the past - whereas his life - was in the present.

He wondered how Becky was and if she ever thought of him or wondered where he had disappeared to. His fleeting thoughts were brought back into check by Matthew, who had accidentally hit his thumb with a hammer; instead of a nail which, accompanied many other nails that supported many mirrors on many walls in the asylum. He cursed loudly while the others laughed, then patted him on the shoulder in a gesture of 'comfort'.

He made sure that it wouldn't happen again as it would take him hours to put up all the mirrors and he had no intention of ending up in the nurses quarters as much as he enjoyed flirting with them. He had work to do and this was of the utmost importance now.

Penelope was still in hospital; in an out of consciousness, occasionally waking to scream and then promptly falling back to sleep again. Her recovery was slow - despite the attention of psychiatrists and an overly-keen reporter for the Mordithax News who was frequently shouted at by disapproving medical staff and was warned to stay out of the building - or the police would be summoned.

Everyone agreed to stay in the library downstairs for the duration of that coming evening and, into the wee small hours. Snacks and hot coffee were provided via the vending machine in the corner of the room, they were free, as Claudia had a key that the engineer had kindly lent her that morning.

Although the coffee was the personification of vileness itself, the chocolate bars were munched eagerly; sustaining their waning energy as the hours ticked by. They discussed their lives as numerous card games were played, with the winners receiving their 'reward' of a packet of crisps and a tot of whiskey that Claudia produced from her rather large handbag - complete with a small bottle of cola for dilution.

There were no sounds in the enormous building, all was still - for now. Pillows and duvets were available for those that couldn't keep their eyelids open, but nobody dared to fall asleep due to the embarrassment of being captured on CCTV in mid-snore, or worse...farting in their sleep! As evening turned into morning, everyone eventually dropped off to sleep. Crawling in the far corner was an ominous-looking greyish-green mist that grew larger and larger as the minutes ticked by... It was ectoplasm...slowly transforming itself into a spirit person.

~CHAPTER FIFTEEN~
A merging of worlds

At 4am, a putrid stench filled the room, waking everybody up from their slumber.

"Jesus, *what* the fuck is that horrible smell?" asked most of them, rubbing the sleep out of the corner of their eyes and focusing their vision in the semi-darkness.

"Either one of you has farted, shit your pants - or it's something *far* worse, if possible!" said Bob, smirking. They glared at him. He apologised profusely - but not with a straight face.

The main light was switched on and they all agreed to have a very early-morning cup of coffee. As cups and saucers were clattered about and the aroma of strong coffee filled the air, Dr Evans noticed that a table and chair at the far left of the room had fragments dropping off it, crumbling onto the floor. A cloud of greenish steam rose off the table and a hissing sound was becoming louder, as the minutes passed.

"Erm, I think one of you had better put your cigarette out as you've left it burning over there!"

Everyone assured him that none of them had lit up a cigarette since last night.

"Then what the hell is causing *that* then?" he asked, perplexed, scratching his head.

"Claudia, go and have a look to see what it is, please," asked the nurses - but she declined. Bob agreed to take a look, so slowly wandered over to the area, his fingers clutching his nostrils together to avoid inhaling the god-awful stench.

As he approached the 'rotting' table and chair, he saw his reflection in a mirror and a figure stood behind him, its arms extending outwards toward his neck. He screamed and ran in the opposite direction. Tripping over a chair leg, he fell into a petrified heap on the floor - looking up into the disfigured face of something that was not of *this* world. It crouched down and gripped him by the neck; choking the words out of his throat, rendering him literally speechless.

As he swung his arms around gesturing to the others to get this thing off him, he felt his shoulder being pulled by Dr Evans and he was dragged across the floor. The disfigured spirit however, wasn't prepared to let go so, it and the Doctor engaged in a tug-of-war struggle with Bob's legs and arms wrenched in two different directions, causing him to scream even louder. Dr Evans reached down into his jacket breast pocket quickly with one hand and pulled out a Bible, shoving it directly into the face of the creature.

"I command you in the name of God to let go of this man!"

The spirit let go and slowly faded from a 3-dimensional being into one of an ectoplasmic mist again. Its terrifying wails echoed throughout the room as it gradually disappeared into the atmosphere. Bob sat up, his face drained of colour due to his frightful experience, his entire body shook violently as he struggled to compose himself. Red fingertip marks were visible on his throat, a trickle of blood travelled down his chest as a grey fingernail had embedded itself within his soft flesh...

The spirit had left its painful reminder of its violent intentions and had ripped itself off in the struggle with the Doctor. One of the nurses tended to the wound and sterilised it immediately, a dressing was applied and Bob calmed down somewhat. Claudia held him in her arms until the shaking subsided; reassuring him with her soothing whispers of love, she told him that everything would be ok and that he was safe now - in her strong arms.

As they all sipped their drinks and a measure of peace descended upon them, from out of the floor, right in the middle of them all, the wooden blocks that it was made from began to splinter and crack. They didn't have enough time to move as the floor opened up before them all. As tables and chairs were tipped over, light reflected off the metal sides of the chair legs and travelled at lightning-speed onto each mirror on the walls.

Horrific faces of spectral beings stared back at them; their heads thrown back as they let out menacing hysterical laughter. Everybody screamed at the top of their lungs - all but one person - Bob. He suddenly discovered a power and a strength within him that he hadn't realized was there before, a courage and ability that overwhelmed him. He began quoting Biblical scripture verses and held his hands up into the air as he did so.

They all knew that he wasn't a religious man, they all knew that he had never read the Bible in his entire life, so *where* was he getting this newfound ability, they wondered. He reached into the chasm in the floor and commanded the spirits to be banished forever from the building. As he looked down into the black murky hole, he saw the face of his ex-wife. She screamed as she reached up to freedom. Many hands were clawing at her face and head as she begged for her life. Claudia's jaw dropped but she felt a pity inside of her that she had never known before. She helped Bob to drag her out of the hole and she landed with a thump upon the hard floor; covered in dust, cobwebs and a sticky oozing green slime. She convulsed, then fainted.

The nurses pulled her towards the far corner of the room by the door and attempted to revive her. Tables and chairs were thrown into the hole and Bob bellowed at the spirits to leave. Enraged and with eyes fixated upon them all, he continued quoting sacred verse.

As the spirits cursed and spouted obscene words back at him, they told him to return back to the past as the young lady who he often thought about, was not who he thought she was.

They also told him to revisit the old witch that resided at the edge of the lane that he had fearfully wandered up recently, she was waiting for him and they had information for him, secrets that would be unearthed - the truth would unfold if he went back.

He looked around and saw Claudia's face; a pleading expression was there, she knew that his curiosity would be too much for him to bear and that he would leave her again. She ran toward him and, as she did so, they both moved a table and hurled themselves into the abyss. The door was unlocked and some ran out; some were sobbing uncontrollably, some were ashen-faced with shock, some were carried out, unconscious.

The spirit faces that mocked within the mirrors snarled and moaned continuously - the terrifying wails echoed throughout the building. Every door in the asylum opened with a sickening creak as a multitude of spirits crawled out of each mirror and prowled each corridor in the huge building. Lights flickered, cameras clicked, night-vision cameras whirred upon their tripods in a frenzy of activity. The temperature dropped instantly; producing a chill that even the coldest freezer on the planet couldn't reach. Every light went out and darkness loomed upon everything.

The elevator door was open...spirits emerged, shouting and screaming angrily. Motion-detecting equipment alarms went off and the trigger object didn't just move, it shot across the room. Blood-curdling screams were heard from the distant areas of the asylum to the nearest corridors that surrounded the staff. Escape from any of the bedlam was impossible.

The front door wouldn't open and the Security Guards couldn't find their guns - rendering them helpless and unable to defend everyone. As if bullets were enough anyway, they thought... Lots of Bibles were thrown across the library, hitting the walls with a loud thud. Some of the staff ran to the canteen to defend themselves with razor-sharp knives, some helplessly gripped the crucifix necklaces that they had around their necks, some prayed and some were simply rendered gibbering wrecks and were totally paralysed with fear.

Time ticked by and silence fell upon the building.

Frantic pulses slowed, hysteria subsided.

Mable told the others that on the other side she had seen another life, another time, when the asylum had been a church, the village was filled with hustle and bustle and trades were busy and villagers were dressed in very different clothing. She had recognised most of them and she had worked in one of the kitchens there and the Reverend would often call in for cups of tea and biscuits after his sermons. She described an old witch that was ostracised and ignored by everyone and, her brother, the Reverend, would keep his distance from the witch as time passed.

He resembled Bob. He *was* Bob, she said. She saw Claudia as a young lady there too and that her and the Reverend had a love that was never fulfilled. They eventually ran away together and the villagers attempted to kill the witch as they had assumed that she were responsible for their 'deaths'. They had erected a stone monument and, after having written about it all - they named it - The Book. The Doctor had discovered it and had hidden it for his research purposes.

Eventually, most of the villagers died in a mysterious fire and after many decades had passed, it was decided that an asylum would be built upon the area that the old church had once stood upon.

It was demolished and the ground was left alone to settle for a while. The stone monument was never destroyed however, and it is now the fountain - outside the asylum. The church had been built upon laylines and the witch had placed a curse upon it that nobody had ever been successful in removing.

When the engineers and surveyors had examined the area before the asylum was erected, they had noticed fragments of mirror that littered the soil and had merely assumed it was from off one of the church walls so they threw them away. One piece had remained embedded within the earth and the building had covered it. Within the fragment of mirror was the spirit of the old witch who had opened a portal to the other side through it via the basement area.

All that she had ever wanted was for people to accept her and to befriend her; to listen to what she had to tell them for their own protection, to protect them from a young lady called Joanne whos' soul purpose was to destroy anything good - to slowly and methodically snuff out the life of everyone; one by one, she was psychotic and very *very* dangerous.

She was eventually discovered wandering around outside the new asylum and was taken in. She has been biding her time over the years and her sole intention is to destroy everyone. Her sister, Jean, also resided there. Mable informed them all that she is extremely observant and psychic but as she feels that nobody believes her - or such things - she keeps her messages to herself.

She reassured them that she is fully aware of Joanne and Jean's evil plottings and, when the time is right she will prevent them from carrying them out. As everyone listened to her, some rolled their eyes in disbelief, some walked away, some let her speak and their minds wandered to their next meal - as it had been several hours since their last one. The hungry among them made themselves some soup and sat in the corner; blissfully unaware that despite the canteen doors being locked, ghostly presences were descending upon that room. Crucifix' were positioned all along the canteen walls and sacred texts were sprinkled with Holy water.

Meanwhile, in Joanne and Jean's securely-locked rooms, they both woke from their sedation and, in a trance, they astral-travelled around the asylum. As they crept up to the canteen entrance, they listened in on conversations. Their bloodshot eyes strained to see inside, through a crack in the door. They bore their teeth, enraged. "They're all going to get it!" Jean growled.

They stood outside the door for what seemed like an eternity as she anticipated their next move. Their matted hair hung around their pale face, fists were clenched in anger. The auric glow surrounding them glowed a blackish-grey. The temperature outside the door began to create slivers of ice that clung to the doorframes that began to suffocate the fibres of the wood; resulting in cracking sounds.

Dampness covered the surface of the stone floor. On the other side of the door, the temperature was just above freezing point; lifted by the halogen heaters that littered the room. The basement ceiling - which was below the library - began crumbling; the plaster and wood fell onto the ground in a multitude of shards, fragments and dust. The hole in the library grew larger and larger, spreading across the floor and bringing every object within the room down with it. The basement elevator door remained open. A deathly-silence wandered around the corridors.

The motion-sensors, despite being activated, malfunctioned. The cameras continued to click and whirr but nothing was captured upon them. Data began to be erased. The trigger object had disappeared. Any evidence of supernatural presence was null and void.

The witch had ensured that not only would she not be captured on camera - or by any other means - she had cleverly enabled the portal to stay open so that she could monitor what everyone in the asylum would be up to throughout the following hours. She had a plan to voice her opinion, and this time everyone would hear what she had to say - for once. She was determined to prevent Joanne and Jean from inflicting harm.

In the distant past, Bob and Claudia found themselves in the village - as it was, all those centuries ago. He showed her around and was astonished to see that the longer they stayed there, the younger they both became. As he found himself standing before her, jaw open, he realized that she was Becky; the young lady that had mesmerised him and who had captured not only his eyes but a part of his heart and *now* he knew why.

He had felt a sense of kinship and familiarity when he had first set eyes on her on a previous occasion and judging by the smile on her face, she had felt the same. She told him that she knew he would return and, if not, she would find him somehow. He was her Jack, but his real identity was - Reverend Charlie Thomas. She had nicknamed him Jack as he resembled her brother.

They decided to go to the witches house and would confront her once and for all - mainly to find out exactly who she was - and to attempt to put a stop to her activities. Many villagers addressed Bob by a different name...Reverend. He told them that they were mistaken, but the bemused expression on their faces told him that *he* was the one confused, not them. He looked down and saw that his clothing was that of a Holy man.

"I'm dreaming again, Claudia", he said. But she knew otherwise. She told him who he was - but he refused to listen to her.

"I've never been religious in my life and I *ain't* starting now!" he said in defiance. "Bob, I mean Charlie, you may not be religious in the future, but in the here and now, you *are*. Embrace and accept it and see what happens."

He held her hand and laughed. "Whatever you say! Now let's go and find out what this witch has to say about it all!"

As they strolled up the dusty pathway, away from the village, she squeezed his hand in reassurance and love, her eyes sparkled with a zest for life and for him. His heart surged with adoration for her and they knew that whatever the future - or the past - had in store for them, they would always find each other throughout the mists of time. They were soulmates.

They approached the old witches house - only to find it burned to the ground. It had been that way for some time it seemed; judging by the appearance of the rubble and timber. They moved some of the blackened wood with their shoes and gazed down at the bones of many dead cats. Feline teeth littered the dry ground and rust-covered oil drums and utensils lay side-by-side and on top of one another like a three-dimensional macabre sculpture.

Ravenous rats crawled across the bones, searching for fragments of charred flesh - only to find none. A steel cross had been erected where the house once stood and old Bibles were scattered everywhere. Crushed cauldrons and pans were piled up; scorch-marks were across them. Empty bottles of Holy water were all over the place; some of the bottles were smashed, some were intact.

"Where the hell *is* she then?" Bob asked, as he looked at Claudia, who's eyes were fixated on the desolation before her.

"Bob, we *must* get back to the asylum. I've a terrible feeling that she may be there..."

"I don't want to go back, Claudia, I mean Becky, I kinda prefer it here and I can live with the outfit."

Claudia persuaded him to return, as the only way that they could find out that truth was to do just that. He reluctantly turned around and they retraced their steps back to their starting point. As they stood outside the old church, they both noticed the corner of a large book emerging through rotten floorboards. It was The Book. Dr Evans must have come back and then had forgotten to take it back with him. Bob wrenched it from the crumbling wood and dusted it off with his hand.

They both sat for what seemed like hours and read every page. As his eyes widened with astonishment, he realized that he had indeed been related to the old witch and that she had been his sister. The Book spoke of her disappearance after the villagers had burned her house to the ground; resulting in her running off. It told of the fire spreading across the fields and burning down houses in the village, causing many deaths. It revealed that he, Reverend Charlie Thomas, had mysteriously disappeared and, the villagers had erected a sacred blessing and an inscription upon stone - telling of the ending of the witches' curse and that the land would from thereon be at peace. They were wrong.

One or two of the villagers that had lived to a ripe old age, had moved to other areas or had died of natural causes. When the church had been demolished, The Book foretold that if any building replaced it in the future, the witch - if she ever returned - would open a portal, a doorway to the other side and, the *only* way it could ever be closed again - was if her brother's remains were found and were scattered upon the ground, all around the foundations of the new building. As a Holy man, this would be the solution; to cleanse the land. Claudia shed tears of sorrow.

"My darling, love can transcend death. Wherever you had gone, I would follow, you *must* have known that I would *never* have left you." Mable often stared at me and I always wondered why. Now I know why, she knew that I was her brother, from the past, but, she never told anyone else - as most of them are sceptical at the best of times and she values her job that much that she didn't risk being ridiculed and mocked." "Come on, let's get back to them all. We can always come back here if you want to, but I'd go to hell and back to find you again anyway."

He kissed her face and wiped her tears away. They opened The Book to the middle and saw a fragment of mirror embedded within it. As they gazed down at the foundations of the new building, he frowned as he saw his ribcage, sternum, spine, laying on the ground on one side, and his femur, pelvic and other bones on the other side of the new building's foundations.

"Bob, what's the matter?" "You can close the portal now." "You gave up your body to cleanse the land!"

"Claudia, there's something missing. My skull isn't here, the portal wont be closed until *all* of my remains are scattered here. We must go back to the asylum and search for it there."

They stared into the hazy mirror and grasped each other's hands firmly. As time sped up, they felt themselves soaring through the decades. Their hair began to grey and wrinkles appeared around their eyes. They smiled and their lips met. Tears of mutual love mingled upon their cheeks as they held each other tightly. In any century, he thought, she would always be beautiful - to him.

"Never let go." they both whispered, as they closed their eyes.

As they walked up to the stone fountain in the grounds of the asylum, they looked up at the greyish-white building and sighed a breath of relief. Ghostly faces glared at them through the windows and they could see all of the staff huddled together in the canteen. The patients had woken up from their sedation and they pressed their noses up against the individual windowpanes, their mouths were open in mid-scream - then stifled, as spirit hands tightened around the soft flesh of their necks.

Glass smashed as their foreheads violently slammed against the windows. Blood spurted everywhere; running down the surface of the glass like a crimson river. Limbs and fingers were torn off as body parts were ripped asunder, sinews and tendons were stretched and then snapped; like elastic bands pulled to their limit and beyond. Hair was yanked out and eyeballs were gouged from their bony sockets.

The face of one of the spirits, its head thrown back in mocking laughter, was devoid of colour and remorse. Others were in frenzied attack, tearing and ripping what remained of any flesh before them. Bob and Claudia ran to the entrance of the building and placed a key in the locked door. As they approached the canteen, Joanne faced them. Bob fearlessly walked towards her and quoted Scripture.

Her agonising screams faded into the atmosphere as she vanished from view. Everyone in the canteen screamed at the commotion on the other side of the door and cowered in the corner of the room, trembling uncontrollably.

As Bob and Claudia marched toward the canteen, Mable stood up and screamed abuse at them. Her face began to morph into a mottled-grey pallor, her usually immaculately-groomed hair billowed out into wisps of dry frizz, her fingernails elongated into sharp talons, her voice deepened.

"So, you found me then, brother!" she hissed. "I *told* you to listen to me a long long time ago, but you didn't. *Now* look what's happened to these poor people - because of *you*!"

Everyone turned to look at her. Some of the staff fainted, some urinated in their underwear as trickles of yellow liquid ran down their legs and spread across the polished floor. Some vomited from fright and shock. The colour drained from other's faces as the full realization of what was occurring, dawned on them. Mable had been telling the truth all along. It hadn't been fictional after all.

"Yes, it's me, sister. I worked out who you were when Claudia and I returned to the village and we saw that your house had been burned to the ground. You had to be

73

somewhere, and The Book led us to you, here."

"All I ever wanted, Charlie, was for everyone to listen to me, to hear what I had to say, but nobody gave me a chance. Not even *you*; my own flesh and blood!"

He walked up to her and asked her what she had wanted to say. Her appearance didn't scare him, nothing scared him anymore. As long as he had Becky back in his life, everything else paled into insignificance.

"I tried to warn everyone of Joanne's intentions. Then her sister joined her, intensifying their powers. She was a powerful and evil dark witch centuries ago, who was hell-bent on destroying everything and anyone that would dare to stand in her way. Her heart is as black as coal and her mind is more evil than you could *ever* comprehend." "I've been watching this place for centuries - to protect you all - *not* to inflict any harm, but nobody ever gave me a chance to tell my story. I've been so frustrated, *so* anguished, so very, *very* misunderstood!" Joanne and Jean control the demonic dark forces...and we are all in grave danger.

Everyone looked stunned. The stench of urine and vomit filled the air and the nurses grappled with towels to wipe up the disgusting mess.

The door handle turned and the glass in it began to splinter and to crack. It flew open and Joanne stood there menacingly. Mable ran towards her and the two witches engaged in a frenzied fight. Dragging each other up the corridor they hurled vile obscenities back and forth as everyone huddled together, watching in horror. Bob ran towards them and threw The Book at them. It landed on Joanne with a sickening thud as it hit the floor.

She screamed as the shape of a cross seared her flesh, leaving its mark upon her forehead. As she slipped away into the atmosphere, her sister Jean following her, Mable, the witch, picked it up and walked into every room, waving it in the air triumphantly. As each malicious spirit launched itself onto her in attack, their painful terrifying wails echoed, reaching into every nook and cranny in the asylum. She slid on the sticky pools of blood that clinged to the floor near the rooms upstairs and she stumbled over body parts as she did so.

Every spirit that confronted her had The Book's holy symbol etched upon them - banishing them back to hell in the process. When none remained, Mable tore the pages out, one by one and set fire to The Book. She scooped up the smouldering ashes and threw them into the gaping hole in the middle of the library's floor.

As each cinder floated downwards into the basement, she cast a protection spell alongside it; throwing salt across every inch of the building and bundles of lit sage as she did so. She returned to the canteen and informed everyone that they were now safe. Nobody believed her of course as they were terrified.

She laughed and informed them that she was a white witch - the good kind. Not like the others who were devoid of any goodness whatsoever.

She resumed her pleasant physical appearance and reassured them that she was a decent soul and that no further harm would come to them. Bob looked at her and for the first time in his life, he believed her. He took her in his arms and sobbed on her shoulder, begging her to forgive him for ever doubting her in the past when he had took the villagers words over hers and had taken their side.

She patted him on the arm and whispered that although she would forgive him, he had one task left unfinished and it had to be carried out. She handed him a large suitcase from behind the cutlery cabinet and unzipped it slowly. He stood there, a confused expression on his face. She reached into the suitcase and pulled out a black plastic bag. Something hard and of a round shape was inside. She handed it to him and he felt hesitant to peer inside. She nodded her head in reassurance and he ripped open the plastic bag. As he held up his own skull, everyone in the room stared in horror.

"Bob, whos' skull is that?" "Does it belong to one of the villagers?"

He looked around at the questioning faces in the room and smiled.

"Actually folks, this is *my* skull and it belongs elsewhere, I'll return it to its rightful place and I'll be back later."

He gazed at his own skull and felt a sense of awe at how wonderfully-made it was and that this is how every person looks when flesh is stripped away to the bareness; so fragile, yet the strength of structural support underneath it all was stronger than metal bars. He admired the honeycomb patterns within sections of the bone.

As he vanished from sight, Claudia explained what the procedure involved and why her and Bob had never been hurt by the witch, Mable. She had only placed her curse upon anyone that wasn't a friend or a relative and who had never an intention or desire to hurt her maliciously. As Bob was her brother - despite not believing in his sister's decency and good heart, she had never intended to harm him - only to lead him to the answers to many questions that had troubled his mind for a long time.

"Mable, I thought you'd sealed up that portal, how did Bob travel back to the past?" the nurses asked.

Mable looked at them and smiled. "When you have the abilities of a witch - or a Holy man, you have special powers of astral-travel, when there is love for others residing within your heart, you have freedom to travel wherever you wish to. There is *no* hell for such ones." "He will be back later don't worry, and then it will all be over and done with and we can carry on with our lives."

She held out her hand to Claudia and placed a silver cross upon it. She advised her to open it up, that there was a tiny clasp attached to it that would open it if pulled. Claudia carefully undid the clasp and looked inside the cross. A pair of gold wedding rings sat inside, glimmering under the canteen ceiling lights.

"My brother has always loved you Becky, but because he was a Reverend in the past - your secret relationship could never be celebrated publicly. Now you can and you are free to do whatever you choose to together. You don't need these rings to cement the bond that you have shared throughout the ages". Claudia thanked Mable and held the rings close to her heart. She gave them back.

"Sylvia, when Penelope regains her full health at the hospital, please give these to her as she can give them to her daughter as she's getting married I hear, this year."

Sylvia told her that she would give them to her when she visited her at the hospital and she put them safely in her handbag.

The police arrived at the asylum and broke the entrance door down. As they ran inside the building, the putrid aroma of decaying flesh and congealing blood filled their nostrils. They raced upstairs and were confronted with a sea of red, dismembered body parts and walls splattered with matted bloody hair and teeth.

They opened each of the patient's doors with the keys from the main office and, in one of the rooms they heard whimpering coming from beneath the bed. As an officer peeled back the blanket from the bottom of the bedframe he saw a sketching pad, crayon and a small trembling hand pushing it towards him. Tricia was alive. Terror filled her eyes and she fought to speak - but was unable.

From out of the corner of his eye, the Police officer noticed a dark presence approaching him. It slipped its claws around his exposed neck. As Tricia thrust the sketching pad into his hands and, his eyes focused on the image before him, he didn't have time to shout downstairs for help... The picture was that of a black circle with a horde of horrific-looking ghostly figures crawling their way from out of the centre of it. A woman stood in front of the circle and, at the bottom of the picture were the words:

YOU FORGOT TO INSPECT THE FOUNTAIN DIDN'T YA...

The officer didn't stand a chance as his head was severed from his torso by one hard twist of the cotton restraint; the metal buckle embedding itself in his shoulder; tearing a long strip of flesh from off his left arm. A red river spat over Tricia as the force of the demon's wrench made its impact. Tricia ran out of the room and skidded on the floor as ribbons of blood poured down her body and onto the ground under her feet. She shrieked as she made her way downstairs as quickly as her sticky legs could carry her, glancing over her shoulder as she did so. Footsteps were heard behind her as she screamed.

Everyone downstairs hurried to get out of the main entrance as they heard the commotion above. As they all ran outside and gathered near the stone fountain, Tricia followed them.

Mable deliberately stayed behind and stood in the doorway. The demon lunged at her

76

but missed - as Mable moved out of the way. It fell onto the concrete steps and hit its head on one of the stone lion statues that guarded the entrance to the building. Sprawled out on the gravel floor, Mable hurled Sacred verse at it. It screamed obscenities in response and vanished into the surface of the ground. Police officers stood perplexed as they stared at the floor.

Mable hurried anyone that was still alive, out of the building, lit a match and threw it into the doorway. Within moments the curtains hanging near the window became engulfed in searingly-hot flames. The police decided not to telephone the Fire Brigade. The asylum took hours to stop smouldering after explosions erupted from the gas canisters in the storerooms and boiler rooms.

As Mable reached into her handbag and pulled out her hand-mirror to tidy up her make-up, she peered into the glass and spotted several demonic entities crawling from out of the centre of the stone fountain. The seal had been moved. One of the horrific dark beings had a wicked smirk appearing upon its face. Baring its sharp bloodstained teeth, it lunged towards the police officers.

Bob walked towards them, followed by Dr Evans and Matthew. They remembered that The Book had been a replica, they had painstakingly copied it, its pages were burnt to cinders in the asylum but, they clutched the original in their hands. The demon turned to look at them and mocked their feeble attempts to overpower it.

"Mere flesh and blood have *no* power over me. I'm your *worst* nightmare and I cannot be stopped so do your worst, fuckers!" it screamed.

Bob laughed, held The Book above the demons head and walked backwards, luring it over to the stone fountain by misleading it to believe that he would sacrifice himself for everyone else. A few days ago, engineers, carrying out renovation work on the asylum and the fountain, had removed the top layer of stone that had covered the inside of it - exposing a dark gaping abyss that gaped, below. Around the edges of the fountain were buttons that activated how high the jets of water would rise from out of it. Dr Evans had replaced the water with Holy water and Mable and Bob had placed a blessing upon that area.

"We may not be able to stop you, you're right, but *God* can"...

As the fountain was turned on, blasts of pure Holy water shot into the air. The settings of it had been adjusted to the point that water would come down outside the perimeter of the stone surround. As everyone felt the cool liquid cascade and splash upon their smoke-stained skin, the hideous demon began emitting sickening eruptions of pus-filled boils, warts and lesions within its body as the water began disintegrating its ghastly flesh.

Steam rose from its limbs and it bore its long razor-sharp incisors as it threw its head back and screeched in convulsions of agony. Bob continued to hold The Book above his head; manouevering the cross upon it around at an angle so that the glassy-encrusted angels that decorated the fountain met the glint of metal from the crucifix; creating a prism of blinding Holy light.

Rays of sacred blessed light surrounded the body of the demon and propelled it toward - and into - the abyss. As it arched its back and screamed, it disappeared down into the gaping depths, its wails and screeches echoed as it fell further into oblivion...and beyond.

As they all gripped the sides of the stone covering and began pushing it back into place - to seal up the fountain - Bob peered into the yawning chasm and a woman's hand reached upward, followed by the pleading voice of a frantic and terrified Mable: "It's me, help me, *now!*" She had thrown herself into the abyss with burning sage and Banishment spells.

He grabbed her hand and yanked her out of the hole. He then threw The Book into the darkness and commanded everyone to seal up the fountain.

"*Nothing* can come back now. It's finished" he said, as he fell to the floor, his sister's arms around him comfortingly.

"Brother, in my long life I've been to hell and back - but never *literally*!"

As they fell about laughing - mostly with relief that they were now safe rather than finding amusement in her joke - lurking behind them underneath the stone seal of the fountain were hordes of demonic creatures trying to claw their way out from the concrete.

"C'mon, let's go and get a cup of coffee at your house. Put some whiskey in mine and Claudia's as we're gonna fucking need it after what we've all been through!"

A demon pushed a small shard of mirror through a tiny gap in the stone seal upon the fountain and a sickening evil grin reflected within it as it watched everyone walk away from the smouldering Ghostly asylum of Mordithax...

"Oh *we'll* be back don't worry!" it growled...as it leafed through The Book and taught itself how to do everything within it - in reverse...

Besides...it wasn't Mable that came back. The sage had been switched by Jean and Joanne previously for mere grass... Impersonating Mable, the Head demon prowled around the grounds of the smouldering asylum...and it could wait.

The Head demon had been the newly-married gentleman - Tim, who had married Victoria, at the Town Hall, centuries before. He was back - for Claudia/Becky.

~CHAPTER SIXTEEN~
Bob and Claudia get married!

It was a quiet wedding. Just a few close friends, some of the staff from the asylum -

and their children, attended the marriage of Bob and Claudia. He had gone down on one knee as she had been slurping a tot of whiskey one evening - spitting it across the room as she heard the precious words come out of his mouth. He took his time getting back up off the ground as hysterical laughter had overcome him, due to her comical response.

"God, you actually made the first move, for once, I'm speechless, Bob!" she had jokingly said. She helped him up off the floor, pulling him toward her ample cleavage. He took his time standing up fully of course and relished the impromptu opportunity to 'worship' her body - even before their marriage vows had been said at the approaching occasion - before a Priest, before they had even signed before the Registrar.

Children weren't on the horizon, they both agreed, as they were getting on in years now and felt that at their time of life - all they needed was each other. Claudia had done her time as a nurse in the past; when she would clean patients bottoms, and she wasn't keen on starting all over again by carrying out the same messy procedure - with a new baby! Bob was relieved as he would be at work all day and would feel guilty if he weren't there to assist her with the upbringing of any children that they bore.

She was enough for him, he thought, she was more than a handful at the best of times - let alone having one or two children in their lives too, to look after. Besides, they both agreed that any time for themselves would be sacrificed - as their time would be taken up with the children.

They enjoyed their times of intimacy too much to be denied that too. It had taken them decades to declare their love for each other - and they both felt that they had an awful lot of catching up to do...

At their wedding, they both had beamed with joy as the priest had announced that they were now man and wife. The wedding rings were of white gold and they had declared their devotion and love for each other in their own words; describing at length how - and why - it had taken them so very long to admit to each other how they had felt for each other, how each had found their soulmate and, an undying love that could rise above anything that life - or death -threw at it.

The limo was a striking violet colour - Claudia's favourite, and, bandages and bedpans were strewn behind the car as it had sped away to their Honeymoon location - Iceland. Bob had always wanted to go there and, during one of their many previous conversations he had told her about ice hotels and hot springs where they could relax and yet be surrounded by ice and snow - while sipping vodka out of glasses made of ice! Their 'towels' were fur dressing-gowns and their 'bedroom' was made entirely of thick icy walls. Bob was mostly looking forward to lazing in the hot springs with her, naked...

During the fortnight, they forgot about everything; about work, stress, reminders of the past. They lived for the here and now and were loving *every* single moment of it too.

When not making love, they strolled arm in arm around the country; stopping off now and again in the car - to admire the stunning scenery. Iceland didn't have much daylight so they made the most of it; taking lots of photographs and generally enjoying the views.

At night, they spent hours conversing about their lives; their childhood and teenage years; laughing at memories of some of the dreadful clothes they were made to wear by their strict parents and, how they snuck out at night to puff on stolen cigarettes that they had cleverly taken from half-empty packets - concealing their theft by moving around the remaining cigarettes in the packets - so that their father wouldn't notice; due to his deteriorating eyesight.

She also told him of when she had been deprived of cuddles and love as a child; it wasn't that her mother and father hadn't loved her, they had, she just always felt from their strict upbringing that this was *her* lot in life too; as she got older- to simply get on with things, best she could, and to be of the same strict attitude to everything - and in how treating others was.

Deep down of course, she was a; shy, kind, gentle soul and, only Bob had noticed it - underneath her stern demeanour, he had noticed a softness and a beautiful soul that deserved love, deserved cuddles, deserved to be shown exactly how special and what a lovely person she really was.

Many of their friends and staff had shed a tear at their wedding as they went into detail about how they had developed their love for each other; spanning decades of; nightly chats, coming to the aid of the other when hurt or frightened about anything and, how they missed each other so very much when they weren't together.

Love really *was* all that *truly* mattered in life. Not how much wealth or power a person has, but how much love resides in the heart and soul. Now they could share this with each other. He had been deprived of affection for as long as he could remember too; bullied at school, bullied in the workplace, ignored by his peers, mocked and generally feeling like an outcast - very unloved. But, Claudia had seen something in him that she dearly loved.

She had ached to demonstrate just how much love for her lived within her heart - but what with her shyness and for fearing of looking silly if he had rejected her - as her parents had - whenever she attempted to have a cuddle from them, only to find arms that wouldn't hold her, she kept her feelings to herself; until she was absolutely sure and one hundred percent convinced that Bob really did love her. Truly cared for her - to the same degree that she did.

If he wasn't the man for her, she would never have revealed her devotion for him but, their longing for each other that night at Mable's birthday party, in the main office, the embrace that they both enjoyed, had shown them that fight all they may, it was inevitable that sooner or later - they would succumb to their mutual love. They complimented each other so well. They always had; and now they always would.

They had smiled at each other as they stood by that Altar; him in his smart suit and dickie-bow, her in her long flowing beautiful violet gown - with a single white rose in her hand - her favourite flower. They would be together in a future lifetime too, they knew. They would be together - eternally. Love is something that all the demons in hell could not destroy. They could destroy a person's physical body - but they would always fail at destroying something that was the opposite to what they were - hate. Love really does conquer all, Claudia and Bob believed. They were living proof of it...

They also knew that they had guardian angels and spirit guides; who looked after them, looked out for them, guided them and protected them. He was *her* guardian angel - in human form, she believed. They didn't need protection spells for their love.

The myriad of glistening icicles that dangled from their ice hotel resembled icy teeth that dripped clear 'blood' and, the rays of sunlight that shone upon them brought out prisms of colour that delighted them.

Staff visited daily to make sure that they had everything that they needed - mainly vodka supplies although, they had sneaked their own enormous bottle of whiskey into their icy hotel - just in case they got withdrawal symptoms of their fond tipple.

Claudia caressed the fur dressing-gown that hugged her cold shoulders as she sat by the edge of the hot spring; dipping her toes into the warm bubbling water, she complained that her bottom cheeks were numb but she was sure that he would warm them up for her! He grinned as he slid around on the ice a few yards away from her while attempting to grab her curvaceous bottom.

"Wow, Bob, you're *such* an impressive ice-skater!" she said as she giggled, gazing into his warm loving eyes as his hand wandered over her body - after she had stopped gasping after his cold fingers had made her instantly shriek.

"I'll have you know, Mrs Thomas, that I used to ice-skate for real in my teens and was exceptionally good at it too, so less of the mocking!" How he loved that sound from out of his mouth - 'Mrs Thomas.' His wife. His heart soared with happiness as he gazed back at her. He felt a lump grow in his throat as he fought to keep a tear from filling his eyes. But *she* noticed. He stood up, skidded around on the ice and composed himself.

"Come here, come and sit beside me, husband", she sighed. They held hands until the sun went down; filling the skies with a multitude of spectacular shades of; orange, pink, red, yellow, purple too- and hues that they hadn't ever noticed before. As they retired for the night - the last one of their Honeymoon, they lay side-by-side and held each other tightly as they snuggled up under their fur blanket. Tomorrow would arrive too soon, they thought, and they felt heartbroken to leave their idyllic haven of icy contentment.

But leave they had to.

For now though, they enjoyed each other's caresses in the night; their mutual adoration and love. Bob lightly touched her fingertips with his as she drifted off to sleep. A tear ran down his cheek as he watched her sleeping peacefully. She was his, now. Truly his. She always had been but, now they were officially man and wife. The pride and love that overwhelmed his heart seemed to be reaching bursting point; as if it would rupture his very soul at any moment. He closed his eyes and held her close, pulling the soft fur blanket around her shoulders.

The next morning, they loaded their belongings into the car and set off to go back home. As they waved goodbye to the staff, they felt sad to leave - but leave they had to. They had no choice. They would forever remember Iceland, with untold fondness.

As they sat together, hand in hand, Bob admired his white gold wedding ring on his left hand as Claudia changed gears. Their thick wool coats kept them cosy as they listened to ballads on the radio. Sipping hot coffee from a stainless-steel flask, he pointed out various interesting things as the car whizzed past.

Their friends, and the asylum staff, waved as they ventured down different roads after all arranging to meet up later that week at Claudia's house, for a huge party.

~CHAPTER SEVENTEEN~
Rebuilding the asylum

Surveyors and engineers assessed the foundations and the structural integrity of the building. Scores of workers; like scurrying ants, milled around the grounds, resting their coffee cups on the ledge of the stone fountain whenever they took their breaks.

"Is that your stomach rumbling again, Harry?" asked Ray, smirking.

"I've eaten, I don't know *what* you're on about mate!" "You need to get your hearing tested, I'm sure you're going deaf in your old age!" replied Harry, his sarcastic wit never ceasing to silence Ray's attempts to irritate him. They had known each other for many years and had been friends at Primary School.

As cement was piled onto the foundations and, additional steel cables were placed to reinforce stability, the arduous task of rebuilding the asylum began. The walls were in reasonably good shape, but the engineers and builders were taking no chances in merely putting new windows back in - the entire building was very old and sections of it had begun to crumble long before the fire had taken hold.

Some of the builders had made the mistake of scraping the charred pieces of mirrors and cleaning them back up - putting them back on the newly-plastered walls...along with the original steel cables that had held the elevator in position. It was an unusually hot week, that week, the sunlight scorched some sand that the builders were using, fusing some of it into miniscule mirrors...

As each window was secured into place - adorned with the most beautiful of satin-lined velvet curtains and, as each corridor was painstakingly painted, the asylum began to gradually return to its original former splendour and glory. Claudia would be very impressed!, they thought.

It took a year before the building was completely finished, which allowed Bob, Claudia, the nurses, security guards and the canteen staff to work on a temporary basis - elsewhere. Besides, it took that long for some of them to get over what they had seen, heard and felt when last there.

As for the others, eternity wasn't a sufficient amount of time for them to *ever* wipe the horrors from their memory. Some decided to stay in a different asylum which was 50 miles away - as they were too terrified to return to the original one, but, the majority of them viewed it as an incident that remained in the past - and that *there* it would stay - buried in the past.

Penelope recovered from her injuries but became too traumatised to do anything really and, as the other one was short of beds, she was transferred back to Mordithax asylum - along with other new patients. Tricia returned. Her artwork had sold at a local art gallery, which boosted her self-confidence considerably. She had blocked out the horrific occurrences from her mind and seemed content, for now. Claudia had framed one of her watercolours that featured the stone fountain and the surrounding trees and shrubbery in the grounds, and she adored the painting. It took pride of place in the main office; where she would allow Tricia to come and view it occasionally.

The following months passed by quite peacefully, nothing unusual happened, everything was back to normal - for now. Mable had found her way back to the asylum via astral-travelling, she had warned everyone about the Head demon that wandered around, but nobody believed her. They tried to reassure her that they had been detained within the abyss of the fountain.

Bob still got jittery whenever he travelled in the elevator - and refused to glance in the mirror. The canteen was back up and running and...lasagne was still on the menu - much to Matron's delight - and to Mable's disgust.

Everyone stayed away from the library for a while and, when they *did* go in there; they went in there in pairs. Just in case... Whenever the ladder moved, pulses raced of the climbees until they climbed back down and set foot on solid ground again. Occasionally lights would flicker during a storm, but the asylum staff would simply refuse to dwell on interpreting it as a paranormal incident brewing and they just put it down to the lightning striking the metal weathervane that perched proudly on the top of the roof.

Thunderclaps made everyone jump, they laughed at their reaction to it with others - mainly to reassure themselves really, that they were not going as crazy - as the patients already *were* and they had no intention of going down *that* road, with them!

The storeroom was bursting at the seams with; new wheelchairs, lavender-infused linen (to aid the patient's sleep and to relax them), electrical irons, ironing boards, reams of paper, a new lawnmower, duvets and spare pillows. Only Bob dared to go in there however and, if any of the nursing staff required supplies, they would ask him to bring them upstairs via the elevator. He wore a crucifix around his neck and always carried a vial of Holy water in his shirt breast pocket - just in case...

Matthew and Dr Evans stayed at the other asylum and would occasionally drive up to Mordithax to see everyone. The Doctor had decided to resume his studies as a Parapsychologist and planned to conduct several experiments over the coming months and years - with Bob accompanying him on investigations. They dared not attempt to conduct one in the asylum as once was enough, they thought. So they would do them elsewhere. They never did find their planchette or spirit board. Maybe they had burned in the fire, they thought.

Likewise, the other equipment had become too damaged to recover; except for the trigger object - a small round hand-mirror, which had been thrown out of a window and had landed in one of the trees outside the building. It was securely-locked within a steel suitcase, kept in a combination safe in the Doctor's office and was never looked into - or exposed to the atmosphere - just in case.

Matron still had her usual nightly tipple - a tot of whiskey, which she shared with Bob late at night. They still chatted in the main office, where she would make him a cup of tea; as they discussed the day's events. He would hold her in his arms as some of the nurses would wolf-whistle through the window at their public displays of affection. After all, they were married now, so they didn't have to hide their mutual devotion anymore. They would simply gesture with a middle finger at the nurses whenever they playfully mocked, grinning as they held the fingers up. The nurses would laugh and then resume their duties.

The whirr of the buffing machines would echo up the corridors as the cleaners shone the floors up to a high sheen; causing the sunlight through the windows to reflect off it with a blinding beam. The cleaners wore black tabards which were complimented by bright-yellow piping all around the edges. As they chatted away, one of them sipped from a can of cola as she manouevered the machine with one hand gripping the handle, thumb on the activation switch.

They had started working there a few weeks before and were unaware of what had happened in the building in the past; having travelled from many miles away. One, who was extremely psychic, had sensed an uneasiness permeating the asylum but put it down to the general creepy atmosphere of the place and the fact that it housed mentally-unstable tortured souls.

The new patients would often wander around in the daytime - shuffling past the cleaners in their fluffy blue slippers like drugged-up zombies, as many of them were sedated most days and, it took a few hours for the effects to wear off. They never caused the staff any problems and were always in bed on time for 'light's out' at 10 o'clock each night.

The stone lions that guarded the entrance to the asylum had been repainted, but the stubbed-out cigarette butt-marks once again defaced them - despite ashtrays sitting upon a table, a few feet away. A collection of used cigarettes piled up at the base of one of the lions; resembling miniscule brown ladders, which ants climbed upward. Ants never wandered into the building as Bob ensured that a light dusting of insect-repellent powder stopped the little army in their tracks.

~CHAPTER EIGHTEEN~
Returning with a vengeance...

Dr Evans had been found stealing pendulums from a shop and had been imprisoned for several months. Sitting on an old wooden stool in prison, picking away at the rusty metal bars that caged him, he shouted to be let out as his paranormal investigations were of paramount importance. He screamed yet another onslaught of abuse at the guards - who simply ignored him - adding to his existing irritation. He would be detained for another week; or so they thought... They could confine him physically, but he had astral-travelling abilities and, no bars in the world could ever prevent that! He had been monitoring things at Mordithax asylum and was biding his time; when he would return, with a vengeance wreaked upon the Head demon. He had discovered what it was planning - and would stop it.

Back in the main office, Claudia was tidying some paperwork and searching for the new patient's Admittance forms. She had a lot to do that day and ticked off each task one-by-one on a chart on the wall, after it had been carried out. She wore a beautiful white satin blouse and a long black cotton skirt under her dark-blue uniform. She looked much younger than her years; mainly due to the fresh lease of life that Bob had instilled into her after being alone for far too long which, had caused her to dress and look much older than she actually was.

As she went outside for her cigarette break, she noticed that the stone seal that lay on top of the fountain had been moved several inches. Her heart leapt in her chest with fear as she walked toward it slowly. A menthol cigarette shook in her hand as she got nearer. A jolt of nausea swept over her stomach as she stood on tiptoe and gingerly looked down into the black abyss. Nothing happened. She breathed a sigh of relief and turned around, rolling her eyes at how silly she had felt.

Standing in front of her was the hazy outline of a woman. She barely had time to recognise that it was the face of the Head demon. Jean stood next to it. She had astral-travelled there from the depths of hell via the fountain - to finally confront Claudia and the others and, this time - she had no intention of leaving!

Claudia screamed at the top of her lungs as the full realisation hit her - it wasn't the 'dead' that she had to be worried about - the dead that were very much alive - and were astral-travelling - were worse! She lunged at Jean to push her out of the way, but she actually ran through her - and an icy chill shot through her entire body. The security guards pushed past each other to get out of the building, guns gripped in their hands.

"Claudia, what the *hell* is the matter? You look like you've seen a ghost!" they shouted.

"Jean is back!" she screamed, as she ran into the building to alert everyone.

The guards looked around - and saw nothing. They burst out laughing as they chatted in the corner.

"Hey look, that seal on the fountain has moved a bit!" They chatted about gambling as they lounged around; still giggling at Claudia's reaction.

As they all approached the fountain, and then attempted to push the heavy stone seal back into place, a mottled, grey arm shot out and the sharp long talons pulled one of the guards into the opening. As he screamed for his life, the other guards pulled his legs backwards. A loud stomach-churning, sickening crunch was heard as his arms were ripped from his torso; spewing gallons of blood everywhere - landing on the men like a red fountain, splattering upon the white stonework in ribbons of sticky wetness and, the demon wouldn't stop until the corpses were drained, one by one.

As the Guard's bones twisted and snapped in the fierce grip of the demon's hand, some of the burly men fainted, some vomited violently on the gravel on the floor, some were frozen to the spot in terror. One urinated in his trousers, the colour drained from his face in sheer fright.

The demon was having a wonderful time; it reached upward and stretched the man's spinal cord, the individual vertebrae began stripping off the spine like a zipper off its fabric 'body'. Its face appeared and, as the sunlight fell upon its features, the men saw the full horror of what was about to be unleashed upon them - and upon the asylum - again...

Bulging red oval-shaped eyes met theirs, scalpel-sharp long bloodstained teeth and a gut-churning growl overpowered their feeble screams, its deeply-etched lesions and pus-filled sores loomed upon them as it forced the stone seal off its opening - as it used the corpse's two legs to prise it off and onto the ground.

Bob looked on from one of the upstairs windows and clapped in approval. Although a decent man by nature, he had a strong sense of justice and believed in the 'an eye for an eye' philosophy - and he believed very strongly in karma.

"Claudia, I don't condone murder, as you know; regardless of whether it's carried out by a human being or whatever other creature, but, those bastards have made my life a living hell of my own, for decades - so no, I'm *not* sorry that they are getting their karma."

"*Why* didn't you come to me, Bob, and tell me just how bad things were with you and them?"

"Because I didn't want to lose my job, and besides, if I told on them...*who knows* what they would do to me then. So I kept my thoughts to myself and just kept out of their way."

They both stood by the window - after locking the door. Only *they* mattered now and their main priority was to stay alive. Once the demon had come into the building, they planned on climbing down the fire escape outside and driving off for good; away from the asylum. If the demon wanted flesh, it wasn't having theirs that's for sure, they thought.

As it stood by the fountain and screeched, others crawled out of the abyss to join it. Most of the Security Guards had been decapitated and, their flesh had been either ripped to shreds or chewed and spat out; gobs of green saliva covered the mangled remains on the ground- like a disgusting multicoloured trifle - gone off, rotting.

As the patients sat in the canteen eating their dinner, they were oblivious of the hellish scene outside. All was quiet in that room, especially as the soundproof panes of glass blocked any sounds from reaching them. Mable saw everything however, as she faced the stone fountain every day. She said nothing and did nothing so as not to frighten the patients who were happily enjoying their meal. They faced Mable, so saw not a thing.

She watched while leafing through her Book of Shadows and Spells that lay on a pull-out shelf underneath the counter-top. As she searched for a Banishing Spell, she silently chanted to the Goddess and to passed-over white witch ancestors; pleading with them to assist in removing all evil from the area. Repeating her requests, over and over in her mind, she felt a sense of relief when she saw a series of Spells that would solve the brutal problem that continued sixty-six feet away from where she stood.

As she rummaged in the cupboards underneath the counter-top, she found exactly what she had been searching for - salt, and sage, - and lots of it. Two main ingredients used in Spellwork. This time, she triple-checked that the sage wasn't grass and, she checked that the salt was genuine - and not mere sugar. Salt was considered sacred and was crucial for the means of protection, cleansing and maintaining positivity in a situation - or for the protection of people under; physical, psychological or psychic attack, from malicious entities or human beings.

She placed bags of it on top of the counter-top and placed the bundles of sage - which were a superb means of cleansing and protecting - especially when burned, and then the flame blown out. A smoking bundle of sage held in the hand of a white witch, was extremely powerful as a tool to keep away any evil - of a paranormal nature or evil thoughts or actions from a physical person.

She placed the lot into a strong brown sack and dragged it out of the canteen, locking the door behind her. Nurses monitored the patients and, despite wanting to vomit at the sight of the carnage by the fountain, turned around and put their attentions to the wellbeing of the mentally-impaired women that sat before them.

They knew of Mable's connections to witchcraft as they had searched for some matches under the counter-top on previous occasions and had come across her Spellbook. As Mable had written notes within the book; about what white witchcraft is, that it has nothing whatsoever to do with the Dark Arts or devil-worshipping, they felt that she was a harmless and goodhearted soul, and so, they left her book alone.

Mable dragged the sack outside, her heartbeat racing in her chest at the impending consequences ahead of her, she telepathically summoned Bob and Claudia to join her. Upstairs, they both sensed at the same time that Mable was in trouble and needed their help.

"Bob, I feel strange, you're going to think that I'm completely crazy but I just heard Mable speaking to me, in my mind!"

"I know, I heard it too! Come on, we can work it all out later, but for now, Mable needs us."

Tricia sat bolt upright in her chair in the canteen and screamed at the nurses to let her out. They refused. She told them that she was a white witch - like Mable, and they had to let her out, *now* - or they would be held responsible for Mable's death - *if* it happened. Not wanting to do that, they decided to let her out. Besides, because of the commotion that she was making, it could alert the demons outside...and they didn't want to be their next meal, they thought, as intestines were hurled at the canteen window as some of the patient's tucked into yards of stringy meaty spaghetti in tomato sauce...

~CHAPTER NINETEEN~
Witches and demons clash!

Mable knew an awful lot about Spells. Being a witch *and* a psychic - like her grandmother, she knew an awful lot about most things; but kept most of what she really felt and thought - to herself. Few people understood witchy-related matters and she didn't want to make the same mistake twice as, in a previous lifetime she had voiced her opinions far too much, causing her death at a fiery stake.

Witch trials were rife centuries ago, many good witches - or white witches as they are correctly called - were put to death, and their crime was?...Healing others, preaching wisdom in the villages as the wise women that they were, they didn't follow conventional 'rules' and were independent souls - not given to 'fitting in with society's expectations', although obeying most laws of the land as peaceable people, they were shunned and feared whenever they carried out spellwork; candle spells were used to bring luck and prosperity to others, herbs and plants were used for banishing bad luck, illnesses or whatever else was requested from them by the believers, but many people felt that witches were an evil sort - so they executed them by fire or drowning or by any other means that they could lay their hands on.

Witches also know an awful lot about spirits - and some know an awful lot about demons too. Mable, Bob, Claudia and Tricia had been of the same coven centuries ago; long before even the church in Mordithax was built.

Claudia had been the High Priestess.

Tricia survived demons attempting to kill her because she had a seal of protection around her. She knew all the rituals, all the methods used to shield oneself from any harm from others. One of the crayons that she drew her artwork with - was usually a black one. She also painted black onyx crystals in her paintings - crystals of protection from negativity -. including that from demons and dark spirits.

As Bob and the three women marched up to the stone blood-stained fountain, they poured out the bundles of sage and the bags of salt in front of the demons.

As Mable opened her Book of Shadows and Spellwork and began chanting, Bob, Claudia and Tricia began pouring salt around themselves and created a sacred circle of protection. The demons growled, flayed hair-matted skin clung from their jaws as they crawled closer to the four of them that stood within the circle. They could smell the putrid breath of the evil spirits, they could see fragments of eyeballs - complete with hanging optic nerves - wedged underneath their long talon-like sharp nails.

They felt the cold chill from off them and saw their eyes; devoid of love or life for that matter. As Mable continued to chant sacred Banishing Spells, the demons began to scream in an agonising mental pain. Their wretched wailings continued for hours as Bob and the women became fatigued and drenched in sweat from the sheer effort of it all.

As the demons faded out of sight and disappeared, Bob dragged the remaining bags of salt around the asylum and created a circle all around the building; blessing it as he did so.

Mable helped Claudia to remember her powers as a High Priestess in a former life and reinforced the protective aspects of the powerful spell. They poured salt down into the yawning abyss within the stone fountain and pushed the seal back over it. Stepping over the bloody bodies of the security guards, they then poured salt on top of the seal. Smoking sage was held around the fountain and verse was repeated.

"It's done." "Now let's have a well-deserved whiskey!" Bob said - as he ran to the asylum entrance. "We can finish the rest of the Protection Spells later!"

After their drink, they resumed their rituals and activities for many hours, ensuring that everything was carried out to their complete and utter satisfaction - nothing less would suffice. It had to be done - properly.

They applied to work at the other asylum; 50 miles away, and to their joy - were accepted. Before that however, a much-needed holiday was on the cards. Bob and Claudia returned to their idyllic icy hotel back in Iceland.

Mable and Tricia went to America to explore the art galleries - accompanied by some nurses who had relatives living there. They didn't want to return but Claudia assured them on the telephone that if they did, a pay rise and a bigger room for Tricia would be available. They returned.

Bob and Claudia took an extended holiday in Iceland and reluctantly returned - after the whiskey and vodka had run out and Bob had developed frostbite on his rather large cock. Claudia did her best to soothe and heal it of course, and he was always *so* grateful for her rapt attention - too much of it he thought - more so at night... He returned to work as Head security guard, a very tired individual. But a happy one.

His cock healed nicely and the nurses often stared at the protruding bulge in his trousers as Claudia had accidentally prescribed him stimulation cream - instead of antiseptic. He found that if he wandered around the corridors holding a clipboard in front of him, his blushes were spared. Claudia found it hilarious however, and would bite her lip to stop herself from smirking; whenever he came to see her in the office.

The electricity supply and all of the fixtures and fittings throughout the building - worked just fine. Nothing was out of the ordinary. In fact, it was rather dull and boring there after a while, so, Claudia decided to spice things up a bit there by having a weekly outing to not just a Flower Shop, but to a weekly treat of food-flinging competitions in a 'wet room' that was built near the bathrooms. Even the nurses joined in as it was surprisingly rather stress-relieving.

She caught one of them smoking indoors on one occasion and promptly threw a bowl of custard over her - reducing her to shrieking hysteria after she had reassured her that indoor smoking was no longer a sackable offence and, the more that she insisted on smoking indoors; the more food she had thrown at her. The nurse gave up smoking eventually.

Claudia continued to wear her seamed nylons; even more so after Bob promised her a boxful of brand-new fancy lace suspender belts and sheer stockings - if she did something about her snoring and farting in bed.

She put a clothespeg over her nostrils at night...and cut down on eating eggs. She had been mortified one day as she had wrongly assumed she were pregnant; but it was a case of chronically-trapped gas in her bowels. She was allowed to relieve herself of this - in their garden, as he sat indoors wetting himself laughing at the comical way she danced around the garden; legs akimbo on the grass as a smile of relief spread across her face. Their elderly neighbour hadn't heard the commotion of course, but he stocked-up on new purchases of outdoor air-freshener and drain-cleaner solutions.

Bob installed an electric fan within their bedroom ceiling - to be on the safe side. She, promised him, a gleaming, brand-new set of spanners, drills and other tools - complete with a shiny new toolbox - if he stopped avoiding making the first move in bed and, took the lead more. He studied books on how to be a better lover. Claudia walked like a cowboy for a week afterwards...

Bob occasionally gave her a piggy-back ride upon his back as way of assistance. He soon put her down though if she farted. Which she did one day, frequently, after mistakingly eating an egg sandwich; instead of a tuna and mayonnaise one, but, as Bob wasn't looking, she carried on eating it until it was all gone.

She had intended on having a tiny mouthful of course, but when things are tasty, it's difficult to stop. Besides, she thought, he hadn't put the toilet seat down one day - so serves him right if I fart, she thought, chuckling to herself; fragments of egg flying everywhere as she snorted a laugh.

~CHAPTER TWENTY~
Is this the end of Mordithax asylum?

Months passed.

Everyone who had left Mordithax to work - and reside - in the other asylum; 50 miles away, gradually began to forget about the past. Life was very different there in the new hospital; compared to how it had been previously, in the other. Birds sang in the beautiful gardens, sunlight shone and, there were *no* stone fountains anywhere to be seen - Matron's orders!

She did however, take the two stone lions with her that she had developed a fondness for as her Bob was the astrological sign of Leo. She ensured that they were cleansed and blessed first - she was taking no chances in transporting any residual bad energy over with her to the new workplace.

Mable loved working in her new canteen - complete with lasagne stricken off the menu - as Claudia had gone off it. The nurses couldn't bear to look at spaghetti in tomato sauce - let alone to consume it, as memories and images of the demons' carnage had etched themselves upon their mind forevermore.

Tricia continued to create her sacred artwork and surrounded the other asylum with pictures depicting; salt, sage, witchcraft symbols of protection and blessing and, she also surrounded the building with granules of black onyx. Sage was hung up near every doorway, salt was sprinkled everywhere on a daily basis - especially in the elevators within the building.

No mirrors adorned any of the walls and all staff were prohibited in bringing their own in - even for the purpose of applying cosmetics upon their faces.

Staff still smoked cigarettes - but Claudia hid the stone lions. She wanted them spotlessly clean and devoid of cigarette butt ends burning the paint from off their gorgeous heads. Bob still got turned-on whenever she pursed her lips around her cigarette as they enjoyed a coffee-break and, she still got turned-on whenever she imagined his toned, muscular body, encased within his pristine-white shirt - which she personally ironed back at their home.

Bob's ex-wife had astral-travelled to him and Claudia and had given her blessing on their marriage - before she was never heard from again. Dr Evans was released from prison and Matthew had found and returned the stolen pendulums after the Doctor had confessed as to their whereabouts. He started to write about his findings while at Mordithax asylum, and his new novel of many was a best-seller. He was to be found a recluse afterwards - due to a constant stream of religious people slandering his efforts to prove that there was an afterlife and that time-travelling and astral-travel were possible.

Occasionally, Claudia, Bob, Mable and Tricia would meet up to keep their coven going, but they would drive many miles away when conducting their meetings - far away from Mordithax - just in case... Just before they had left the place, as several trucks had emptied hundreds of barrels of salt onto the foundations of the asylum, and a ton of smoking sage was thrown upon it also, High Priestess Claudia, Bob, Mable and Tricia - powerful witches from a previous life - *finally* ended the evil that had descended upon

The ghostly asylum of Mordithax.

The demons, villagers from centuries ago, evil-minded patient's and the Head demon were unable to wreak havoc any longer.

The other asylum was painted a cheery yellow shade and the walls and corridor floors were of a pleasant pink hue. Everyone felt, and agreed, that this was the way to go - as nothing in the building would be even the *slightest* reminder of Mordithax asylum. Instead of a stone fountain in the grounds, it had rose bushes scattered everywhere - in every colour of the rainbow. White were Claudia's favourites however; after Bob had presented some to her every morning, with a soft kiss upon her hand.

She began insisting that all staff - including herself - would wear black uniforms, with green piping around the edges, and they would all wear a black onyx crystal around their necks. Any staff that refused to do so - were immediately sacked from their employment.

The weeks and months ticked by and Claudia decided that the elevators would be removed entirely from the building. This pissed the staff off of course, as they would have to rely on climbing the stairwells several times a day. Their leg muscles toned-up dramatically - thereby allowing them to cancel their subscriptions to the local gym.

The patients were escorted out of the asylum, once a month, onto a waiting train; to take them to the city of Styfea, where they wandered around, enjoying the shops, cinemas and antique shops to their heart's content.

When one of the patients had made the mistake of picking up a hand-mirror, Matron had yanked it out of her hands immediately - placing it back down upon the table and hurriedly marching the woman out of the shop!

In the city of Styfea, in the many cafes and restaurants, Mable avoided lasagne that seemed to constantly be 'dish of the day.' She had seafood instead. Claudia, however, relished lasagne and would mull it around on her tongue while staring at Mable, childishly. Mable would respond by kicking her under the table - and then apologising profusely - while winking at her and flinging a prawn at her.

In the winter months, they all enjoyed the experience of ice-skating; Bob still held onto the walls and skidded as Claudia glided around on the ice gracefully - pinching his bottom as she sauntered past. He would attempt to follow her - but fell flat on his backside, often, much to her amusement. He had a bruised, sore backside for three days, which she lovingly tended to in bed at night - slathering him in soothing deep-heat cream.

He turned the heating down in the bedroom, frequently, as she lay there shivering. He would console her by cuddling up to her and, one evening, he had silently slide his hand down to her clitoris - complete with a globule of the very warming cream, on the end of his finger. She threw the cream out and never went ice-skating with him ever again.

Back at Mordithax, the bricks and steel structures that had supported the building were crushed into dust and burned under the sacred light of a full moon. Mordithax ran out of salt, and sage, and had to have fresh supplies shipped-over from abroad, where it lay in a newly-erected large outdoor storeroom.

The area where the asylum had once stood, was turned into a giant cinema. People travelled from miles around to watch all sorts of films; it was a cheery place once again as visitors enjoyed the other newly-built buildings also. There was a; flower shop, butchers, lasagne restaurant, a police station, a cemetery was strewn with colorful posies and bunches of roses - except for several unmarked graves which became hidden from view over time as the grass was allowed to grow over them.

There was a stone monument erected; to remember all the dead - those that had lost their lives there - and those that had been murdered by the demons but, this wasn't mentioned on the monument at all; the details had been left off it completely. The inscription described a mysterious accident that had occured there - and visitors were left bemused as to exactly what had gone on there. Relatives of the dead however, paid their respects, and sat for a while, staring at the empty space where the asylum had once stood - and what had gone on there.

Claudia had told them all about it at their individual homes. Some believed her, some refused to do so. The police intervened and Claudia had been advised to steer clear of their houses indefinately.

Mable, Bob, Claudia and Tricia paid one final visit to the place; to say goodbye to the staff that had been killed, the patients that had been murdered in their beds and, they said their goodbye to the building itself; a place that they had devoted many decades to in service, an asylum that contained many positive and happy memories - despite the others, that weren't.

They shed a tear each as they stood, hand in hand, gazing at a derelict reminder of hard work, healing, parties, a place where two of them had finally admitted - and consumated their mutual love within, a place that they once loved. Demons could never erase the good memories, they thought. They took innocent lives there and destroyed the peace but, they could never destroy everything that had once been; pleasant, the friendships that had been forged there, the sheer devotion to medical procedures that they had adhered to - to help others.

A new life began in the other asylum, a new time to live life to the full; with a spirit of; optimism, joy and positivity. Claudia wouldn't stand for any sulleness within the workplace and, would sedate any patient that depressed her. She felt for them of course, and their predicament of suffering from clinical depression - she just didn't want to be around it, so, she was often found in the main office; rather than the patient's rooms. Bob spent a lot of time there with her; which helped her enormously to overcome the unending post-traumatic stress disorder that kept her awake most night's. He comforted her at these times but, he felt anxious for the state of her mind quite often.

"I hope to God that you don't *ever* end up admitted as a patient, my darling," he had said to her on one occasion, to which her reply was; "Not bloody likely!"

She gradually recovered and her mood lifted quite dramatically as time went on. Bob was relieved beyond words when he witnessed her transformation into that of a depressed, jittery woman, into one of her old self; a glittering sense of humour combined with a zest for life - a life with him.

His eternal adoration for her and undying love had brought her back, it had saved her, it had destroyed what he had feared - her losing her mind. He couldn't bear that. He had lost her once, he wasn't going to do that again. Wherever her mind had wandered - if she had lost it - he would find her in the mists of time, he would bring her back again.

In the weeks that followed, Claudia had the task of welcoming new patients into the asylum. She filled out the usual forms for their relatives to sign, she greeted each of the patients and got to know them, she showed them around the building - and which of the areas that they were prohibited from exploring and, she chatted with their relatives to find out everything that she could about their history, medical conditions, and so forth.

She was an excellent Matron, always had been, but she vowed to be an even better one in the new asylum. She would ensure, along with her rediscovered witch powers, that no harm would come to anyone in the building.

Mable often walked past her and bowed to her in a gesture of respect - whenever nobody was around - she addressed her as 'High Priestess' and Claudia smiled in return. Their friendship was strong now, they respected each other and all that they stood for; healing, helping, protecting.

Dr Evans and Matthew had requested a visit to the asylum - to inspect and to explore it - but, Matron had denied them access via burly security guards weilding guns. Claudia told the Doctor and Matthew that they would converse with them in a different town - so as not to stir paranormal activity up again; despite his pleadings of promising to ensure the safety of everyone in the asylum. Bob told him that if he wanted to explore any buildings, to investigate them on a paranormal basis, then he would have to go elsewhere.

The Doctor reluctantly went along with this suggestion. Matthew repeatedly warned him of the serious consequences if he ignored it. They both investigated other buildings, but they didn't gain as much interest - or enjoyment from them as they would have if they had been allowed access to the asylum. Dr Evans retired, eventually and, Matthew got to know Mable while meeting up with her in the restaurants in the city. They realized, to their surprise, that they had a lot more in common than previously thought, and a few months later they got married.

Dr Evans was last seen hobbling around on a walking stick. His eyesight began to fail him in time, so he was admitted to a nursing home where he would be heard chatting incessantly about; ghosts, demons, missing pendulums and the like. The nurses would humour him, but would walk away - shaking their heads in confusion, assuming that senility was looming upon him in due course.

When Claudia, Bob, Mable and Tricia had carried out the Banishing and Protection Spells previously, by the ruins of Mordithax asylum, Bob's skull had completed and had sealed the final Protection Spell, as he had travelled back in time to 1714 and, as he had returned to 2034, to the asylum, from the old church, nothing evil could ever descend upon Mordithax again. History wouldn't repeat itself.

Well, not unless another witch reversed it, perhaps and, in the other asylum, a new patient was to be admitted there within the coming month.

She was a relative of Joanne and Jean...and she insisted on wearing a crucifix around her neck - upside-down... Claudia couldn't sack her as she was a patient. She sat with the family of the woman and convinced them that there simply wasn't sufficient room at the asylum for her - she lied. The family bought this excuse, so, she was sent to a different asylum - 1,000 miles away - far enough away not to bother them physically. What they hadn't banked on though, was her powerful abilities to astral-travel...

Dear reader, please consider writing and leaving a little review on Amazon for this paranormal horror novel as your review will help not just the author but it will help and inform potential readers also. Feel free to tell your friends about the book too, so that they can read it. Thank you.

Check out the author's other existing books on her Amazon author page. She writes and publishes stories on a regular basis in several different genres to entertain readers worldwide.

Take care and have a great day!

CPSIA information can be obtained at www.ICGtesting.com
Printed in the USA
LVOW04s1846070715

445299LV00032B/2457/P